TO DEFY A HIGHLAND DUKE

Heart of a Scot
Book Six

By
COLLETTE CAMERON®

Blue Rose Romance®

Sweet - to - Spicy Timeless Romance®

USA Today Bestselling Author
COLLETTE CAMERON
Sweet-to-Spicy Timeless Romance®

For permission requests, write to the publisher at the address below.
Attn: Permissions Coordinator
info@collettecameronbooks.com
collettecameronbooks.com
eBook ISBN: 978-1-954307-78-0
Print Book ISBN: 978-1-966087-40-3

FREE BOOK!

JOIN MY EXCLUSIVE MAILING LIST
Collette Cameron Newsletter

AND GET A FREE EBOOK!

https://collettecameronbooks.com/freegift

Plus Sneak Peeks, Giveaways, Contests, Exclusive Content, and More... P.S. I promise only good stuff ~ **no** spam!

DEDICATION

For castle, coffee, and cat-lovers alike.

ONE

Scottish Highlands
29 December 1720

I'm out of my mind for agreeing to this. Completely and utterly mad.

With that peevish thought, her fingers ice-cold despite her gloves, Marjorie Kennedy shivered and burrowed further beneath the weight of the heavy coach blankets. Only the crown of her soundly sleeping daughter's head peeked from within the cocoon she'd swaddled six-year-old Cora in.

On the opposite seat, her sister-in-law, Berget Kennedy, also buried in a swath of thick coverings, cuddled Elana, Marjorie's seven-year-old daughter.

The bricks now skidding around the coach floor had long since lost any semblance of heat and had been abandoned as foot warmers. Wishing for a roaring fire to warm the soles of her feet, Marjorie wiggled her cold toes against the bottom of her sturdy shoes.

"I canna imagine 'tis much farther, Marjorie." Every bit as exhausted and miserably cold as she, Berget offered a weak upward sweep of her mouth, empathy shining in her kindly gaze. "The last time we stopped, Graeme vowed we'd arrive within the hour."

With chipped teeth, bruised bums, and our blood frozen solid.

Well, Berget might not be frozen through and through. Her bright eyes and flushed cheeks, and the smoldering glance her husband bathed her with when they'd emerged from the inn's private parlor, suggested Graeme had found a creative and effective way to warm his young bride.

Overseeing her daughters' use of the necessary behind the posting house meant Marjorie had never completely thawed before the troupe reboarded the coach and lurched away on the rutted excuse for a road.

It wasn't precisely envy that pricked her, for she didn't begrudge Graeme and Berget their happiness or love. True, Graeme resembled her dead husband Sion strongly and, for a brief period, she'd developed a *tendre* for him.

But the sentiment hadn't been love. He'd reminded her so much of Sion, and she did so miss her husband.

So, *what* precisely, was this disgruntlement chafing her? Abrasive and persistent.

If she must put a name to the aching, fluttering behind her breastbone, she'd call it yearning. For what she'd once had and mightn't—*probably wouldn't*—ever have again: the love and devotion of a strong, loyal, devoted husband and father.

Could one grieve such things?

Love. Devotion. Companionship.

Should one?

How could she not?

Her heart and spirit had wills of their own these days.

Burying her fingers deeper in the furs, Marjorie attempted to ignore her discomfort while keeping her complaints constrained to mutinous musings. Vocalizing her displeasure served no useful purpose, since naught could be done but endure the remainder of the bone-rattling trip.

Besides, it wasn't her nature to be churly or snipe.

This journey, however, reinforced her abhorrence of coach travel, which was why her last prolonged trip had been from England as a bride of eighteen. Starry-eyed and bubbling with hope and expectations as the young bride of Laird Sion Kennedy.

She'd been blessed with three and a half joyful years with Sion before he'd died, far too young, five years ago. Her brawny, strapping husband felled by a gash. A stupid infection of his foot that had turned putrid and poisoned his blood, claimed the doctor.

Sion had left her a widow at two and twenty, in a new homeland, with an infant, a toddler, and a shattered heart and broken spirit. Her daughters were what kept her going.

Maternal pride blossomed in her chest as she swept a love-filled gaze over the sleeping lasses. Thank God for Elana and Cora. She didn't know how she would've borne the grief and loneliness without them.

The constant rumbling, jerking, and bouncing of the coach had whittled her mischievous daughters' good humor to grumpy pouts and, eventually, frustrated tears before slumber claimed the pair. Experience had taught Marjorie that they would awaken energized and quite ready to engage in more shenanigans.

For certain, the propensity for impishness came from their Scots blood.

"I'm quite looking forward to a hot bath and a steaming cup of tea," Marjorie admitted, realizing she'd forgotten to respond to Berget. Tiny, frosty puffs accented her words and emphasized precisely how frigid the temperature had become inside the coach since the sun began its slow descent behind the Highlands' craggy horizon.

A tot of bracing brandy or whisky in the tea wouldn't go amiss either.

"Aye, I do too," came Berget's muffled reply.

Hours of trundling along in this inhospitable weather had chilled Marjorie to the marrow. A glance out the coach's window revealed a cranky, charcoal-gray sky. She pulled her mouth downward and leaned forward a couple of inches, then clamped her teeth together in another bid to tamp down the wave of frustration billowing upward from her chest.

Perfectly wonderful.

If she weren't mistaken, and she'd lived in the Highlands long enough to know she wasn't, those pregnant clouds portended snow.

Had Berget noticed too?

Mayhap that accounted for the single crease between her russet brows, the only indication she was less than satisfied. Berget hadn't uttered a word of protest during the lengthy journey, and she'd been traveling longer than Marjorie. Her sister-in-law was a saint and had become a good friend in recent months.

She and Graeme had returned from Liam and Emeline MacKay's Yuletide house party to collect Marjorie and her daughters for the trip to Trentwick Castle.

Marjorie sincerely believed she would've been half-mad by now had she been required to jostle about in a conveyance as much as Berget had the past few months.

And yet her sister-in-law remained as cheerful and patient as ever. Marjorie couldn't help but admire her daughters' former governess's stamina and good nature. It was no wonder Graeme had fallen in love with Berget.

Fending off the beginning of a headache, Marjorie pressed

two fingers to the bridge of her nose and wondered for the umpteenth time why she'd agreed to spend Hogmanay at Trentwick Castle.

Not just Hogmanay, but a full week of festivities, God help her. A week amongst strangers. More on point, in the home of the Duke of Roxdale.

Loneliness and boredom, that's why.

Pshaw. She silently but emphatically disregarded the impudent thought. *Utter twaddle.*

She was the mother of two adorable, vivacious daughters, and she lived with her charming brothers-in-law, Graeme and Camden Kennedy, kind-hearted Berget, and a good-sized, devoted staff.

She most assuredly was neither lonely nor bored.

The pair of red-haired minxes currently—*blessedly*—sleeping soundly made certain of the latter. As for the former? Well, Marjorie refused to contemplate it. Widows with high-spirited daughters had other things to occupy their time and thoughts.

Neither, however, was she contented.

Eyeing the pewter, slightly pink-tinged sky, she schooled the frown once more trying to pull her mouth downward at the corners. Most definitely snow. Marjorie almost rolled her eyes heavenward in silent rebellion.

Had that devil, the Duke of Roxdale, summoned the foul weather? *Nae.* Devils preferred roaring fire, not snow.

Despite her determination otherwise, a sigh filtered past her lips.

All they needed was to be snowed in with the austere, ill-disposed Keane Buchannan, Duke of Roxdale.

To think, last summer—*for all of five foolish minutes*—she'd believed him disarming and interesting. *Before* his true colors had emerged. Rather, his true personality. Surly. Dour.

Judgmental. His midnight severe brows pulled together and thunderous censure heavy in his arrestingly beautiful hazel eyes.

The devil cannot have beautiful eyes, she argued to herself.

No? Well, that one does.

Probably to enchant his victims into sinning like the sly serpent in the Garden of Eden.

With deliberate intent, and perhaps the merest thrust of what she considered a too-square chin, Marjorie pointed her thoughts in another direction and stared out the grimy window.

In the freezing mist, she could make out the outline of Graeme's huge horse plodding along to the right of the team.

Always mist and fog and rain and gray. Yet, she'd grown to love the Highlands.

Her brothers-in-law preferred to ride, rather than stuff their large frames into a cramped coach. Not that she blamed them. Towering well over six feet and boasting legs and arms to rival small trees, each was as out of place in a conveyance's small confines as an elephant in a canary cage. But surely, they must be half-frozen themselves, even if they were Scots and accustomed to the cold clime.

A particularly powerful shiver scuttled up Marjorie's spine, spreading across her shoulders and raising the flesh. Shuddering, she silently cursed the weather, her sense of duty, and, most of all, the domineering man she'd encounter all too soon.

Come now, she chided herself, *are you going to allow the likes of that bounder to keep you in a temper?*

Aye. The duke abraded her worse than scraping her naked bottom upon splintered wood.

Hunching lower in the blankets' folds, Berget offered a sympathetic smile.

Marjorie's frustration must've shown in her expression despite her efforts to appear unperturbed.

Trentwick Castle cannot be much farther. It cannot. Marjorie hoped as she clamped her teeth against another shiver and burrowed into the furs pulled to her ears.

This gathering would be the first time the feuding Kennedys and Buchannans had marked Hogmanay together in over three decades. Roxdale's father had impregnated Graeme's aunt, and Gordan Buchannan had been forced to marry Winifred Kennedy at blade point. She'd been as reluctant a participant as the old duke.

According to Camden, family lore claimed his aunt had wept copiously throughout the ceremony and, all the while, the fifth duke had vehemently vowed he'd never bedded the lass. She'd died a mere month after giving birth to Roxdale—some said from a broken heart.

Roxdale's strong resemblance to his sire—the entire ducal lineage, in truth—refuted the old duke's adamant claims that he hadn't fathered the bairn.

Henceforth, the families had avoided each other. Until now.

And she was to blame, in part.

Blast her interference and attempts at peacemaking.

TWO

Marjorie had encouraged Graeme to invite Roxdale to the *cèilidh* festival last August. *Yes, and look where your insistence has landed you?* she scolded herself. Freezing, dreading the upcoming week, and forced to be gracious to their brusque, curt host who'd soundly insulted her the last time she'd seen him.

Nonetheless, in recent months, Graeme and Roxdale had decided to put past offenses behind them and, as the former laird's widow, Marjorie felt it her duty to attend the house party. Even though Roxdale's behavior when they'd last met was nothing short of appalling.

She winced slightly at the offending memory, seeing that day as clearly in her mind as if it had been yesterday. She closed her eyes to block out the intrusive recollection, but to no avail.

Cora and Elana, their little cheeks stuffed squirrel-like full of clootie dumpling, had giggled hysterically while they talked, causing a spray of crumbs to fly forth onto the table. They'd never been deliberately ill-behaved before. Apologizing to Roxdale, Marjorie couldn't hide her dismay and mortification.

Eyebrows arched in a superior fashion, he'd sternly criticized her daughters' table manners before she had a chance to gently correct them. It hadn't been his place to admonish the girls. His cold disapproval meted out in clipped, critical tones had reduced Cora and Elana to tears.

Nor had it been his place to reprove her and remark on her shortcomings as a mother. *Oooh*, even now, her blood heated. He'd all but implied she was an empty-headed nincompoop incapable of properly raising her daughters.

It only happened rarely, but Marjorie had lost her temper, giving credence to redheads' reputations for having fiery temperaments. Fury goading her outrage, she'd whispered in his ear in similarly starchy syllables as his own precisely what he could do with his opinions and admonitions.

Her suggestion may have contained a reference regarding what cavity into which he could stuff his handsome, arrogant head. And perhaps another reference to said head being so inflated with self-importance and self-righteousness it wouldn't fit in said cavity.

She might've also asserted he wasn't so different from the other ignoble blackguards who'd held the title before him, and she'd been grossly misguided in badgering Graeme to invite him to the celebration.

His features chiseled from granite, Roxdale's hazel eyes had gone cold as steel. Wordlessly, he'd risen, sweeping a condescending gaze over Marjorie and her daughters. He took her measure, inch by insolent inch. Given the snide tilt of his lips, he'd found her wanting.

One of his raven brows had shied upward, just this side of contemptuous, and she'd balled her fists and bitten her tongue to refrain from telling him in front of her daughters to bugger himself. Stiff-shouldered, his anger and derision palpable, he'd strode away, his strapping legs moving with lithe grace that a man his size should not possess.

And a woman as peeved at him as she was had absolutely no business noticing.

Later, Marjorie had learned Cora and Elana had been mimicking the antics of a pair of rascally clan Buchannan lads who were sitting behind her and the duke. Nevertheless, the girls washed dishes for a week for their discourtesy.

She'd contemplated requiring them to write Roxdale notes of apology. But then Roxdale's proud, angular features arranged into a derisive mien sprang to mind, and instead, she itched to slap the superior smirk off his lovely, sculpted mouth.

Lovely, sculpted mouth?

Had she gone mad?

No. No. That was not what Marjorie meant at all. *His smug mouth.* Yes, indeed. Smug and seductive as sin.

Another unwanted memory of that day played around in her mind: when the *cèilidh* dancing had commenced in the evening.

Even now, humiliation scorched her cold cheeks at the unwelcome recollection. Her face probably glowed like candied apples. Thank God the coldness inside the coach could be blamed for the high color.

She slid Berget a covert glance, gratified to discover her sister-in-law had closed her eyes once more. Poor, exhausted dear. She must be wholly done in due to traveling so many days on end.

Marjorie unwisely permitted her mind to replay those last few moments with Roxdale last August.

Quite naturally, Graeme had partnered his new bride for the first dance. Which meant, according to custom, the next highest-ranking male and female should dance together. Determined to be gracious and forgive Roxdale his earlier offense, she'd faced him with a friendly, expectant smile on her face and awaited his request.

It never came.

The utter boor had declared *he* didn't dance and turned his back on her, leaving her standing with everyone slack-jawed or whispering and shuffling in discomfiture. *Liar.* He did too dance. She'd seen him compete in the sword dance earlier.

In fact, she grudgingly—*very grudgingly*—admitted the duke was a bloody fine dancer. Agile, unexpectedly elegant, in absolute control of his sinewy form and movements. *Yes, a damn, bloody brilliant dancer.* And he'd publicly snubbed her.

What he'd clearly meant was he didn't want to dance with *her* after the uncomfortable incident with her daughters.

Ever chivalrous, Camden had sprung to her rescue, leading her to join the other assembled dancers. Throughout the set, he'd murmured reassurances while making aspersions about Roxdale's parentage.

Which, in truth, insulted Camden's unfortunate aunt.

Enough! Do not spare the knave another thought.

Peeved that she'd allowed him so much contemplation, Marjorie pointed her toes up and down, up and down, and released a long, silent breath through her nose.

Why must she keep ruminating about the odious Duke of Roxdale?

Well, because, quite frankly, within minutes she'd have to plaster on a polite face and greet the pompous oaf.

In truth, she wasn't sure she was up to maintaining the façade an entire week. Eight days to be precise. It would tax her resilience and fortitude, but if it killed her, she would be an example for her daughters. And she'd represent Clan Kennedy in the manner the noble tribe deserved.

As vexing as it was to admit, she'd lost her temper within

fifteen minutes of meeting him last summer. She, who seldom indulged in displays of anger.

What would a week in his proximity do to her usually mild nature?

Marjorie shuddered to contemplate it. For her daughters' sakes, she must put on an air of indifference.

At last, the coach bounced and jarred to a rocking stop before an impressive stone keep. Charming in a medieval, rustic way, Trentwick boasted three turrets: one on either side of the E-shaped main structure, and another high atop a rectangular tower. In the fading light, and with the ash-tinged, low-lying clouds shadowing everything, the castle had an almost mystical, fairy-like air about it. And the majestic turrets towered over it all, stoic sentinels keeping diligent watch.

Far better that than eerie.

Except she well knew no fairy folk resided within the stately structure. Nae, Satan's spawn called the castle his home.

The girls had stirred when the coach ceased moving and, after yawns and rubbing their eyes, eagerly peeked from the windows.

"'Tis verra big, isna it, Mama?" Cora asked, her nose flattened against the smudged glass.

"Indeed," Marjorie agreed with sincerity. Trentwick was significantly larger than Killeaggian Tower, Graeme's keep and their home.

Elana sniffed disapprovingly and screwed her eyes tight. She hadn't forgiven the duke for his harsh reprimand.

In truth, neither had Marjorie.

"I think *our* castle is much better," Elana muttered unimpressed, sounding like a true Kennedy. "Our gardens and stables too. I bet their cook isna half so talented as ours. She probably burns the shortbread."

A most serious offense, indeed.

A few heartbeats later, the women and children descended from the coach, and Marjorie took in the surroundings. Well-maintained grounds and buildings met her initial inspection. Pity that. She'd hoped he was a negligent laird. Perhaps his singular flaw was his critical, opinionated temperament.

In a blink, Graeme scooped Cora into his arms, and Camden did the same with Elana.

Marjorie held no doubts regarding her brothers-in-laws' devotion to their nieces, and her daughters adored their brawny uncles. The girls giggled as the doting men swung them high, then pretended they were going to drop them.

Elana scarcely remembered Sion, and Cora didn't recall her father at all. Marjorie's heart twinged at that painful truth.

Graeme and Camden had become proxy fathers—another reason Marjorie promptly dismissed the notion of leaving Killeaggian Tower whenever it crept into her mind.

Which, if she were honest, happened more and more of late.

Now that Berget had taken over the duties as mistress, as was her right, Marjorie had little to do. And idleness was a dangerous thing. Inactivity and boredom caused ruminations, and ruminations beget discontentment. Discontentment led to impossible, improbable, and implausible wishes and dreams.

Shaking off her morose ponderings, she formed her mouth into a genial curve. It seemed she was always smiling to disguise her true feelings. And no one ever noticed the sadness behind the façade.

Affection glinting in his gaze, Graeme shifted Cora to one bulging, oversized arm, and wrapped the other about Berget's trim waist. "I trust ye dinna suffer too much, my love."

"Nae worse than ye." Berget's mouth formed a devoted

smile as she eyed him up and down, seeking any sign he might be unwell or suffered ill-effects from his ride. "I dinna ken how ye could stand ridin'. I was freezin' in the coach."

He kissed the tip of her cold-reddened nose, then reared back. "Odin's teeth. Yer nose is cold as a well-digger's ar—"

Berget coughed behind her hand, giving Cora a pointed look, and Camden chuckled as he chucked Elana beneath the chin.

"I'm no' sure that's a complimentary comparison, Brother," Camden said, a taunting grin splitting his face.

"Uncle Camden," Elana squealed and, amidst giggles, attempted to chuck *his* chin. He lowered her to the ground as Graeme did the same with Cora.

Marjorie stifled a groan as she pressed her hands to the small of her back. Eyes closed, she arched her spine and neck. Would it be rude to request a hot bath the moment she entered Trentwick? Preferably with lavender and chamomile oils.

Aye, it would, but if doing so meant postponing greeting their austere host—

A cold, icy splat landed on her nose, and, eyes yet shut, she lowered her upturned face.

Wonderful. Just wonderful.

As she'd feared, the snow had arrived and sifted from the sky in large, wet, fluffy flakes.

"Snow!" Cora crowed in delight. "Mama, 'tis snowin'."

Another heavy snowflake plopped onto Marjorie's cheek, swiftly followed by another and another.

Her eyes flew open, and she found herself staring straight into the Duke of Roxdale's searing, dark-honey gaze. An undefinable force ignited between them, holding her immobile.

Six feet, four inches of raw, inscrutable masculinity, he stood on the entrance's lowest step. Not that Marjorie gave credence to such blatant, predatory maleness or overt confidence and indolent pride.

His mouth twitched the merest bit before his focus dipped to her still upward thrust breasts—*oh, my God*—and that sinful mouth most definitely arched upward.

He leered at her in front of all and sundry, the despicable scunner.

Her mouth gone dry, Marjorie was still incapable of moving or speaking. And, bless the saints and the angels, something more than offense and outrage held her immobile. Enthralled. Intrigued.

Move. Say or do something before someone notices.

Smiling that vexing and damnable smoldering smile, Roxdale directed his focus to her cavorting daughters. Laughing, Elana and Cora romped about, attempting to catch snowflakes on their tongues.

That spurred Marjorie out of her reverie.

The beast.

At once, she straightened and gathered her plaid closer.

The tiniest tingle of pleasure still trilled through her. It had been a very long while since she'd seen that particular glow of appreciation in a man's eyes directed toward her.

She held out her hands. "Girls. Come here, please."

After shooting Roxdale a wary glance, they obediently scurried to her side and clasped her hands, the epitome of demure, well-mannered lasses.

Well done, my darlings.

She couldn't prevent the half-smile she permitted herself, even as she looked at a point behind him.

"Welcome to Trentwick." Roxdale's low, melodious brogue carried to her as he swung his attention to Graeme. He extended his arm for his cousin's hearty clasp. He then gripped

Camden's forearm before dipping his head toward Berget. "Lady Kennedy."

"Your Grace." Although surely stiff from the journey and cold, she dipped into a pretty curtsy.

Lastly, he turned those enigmatic hazel eyes on Marjorie and her daughters. Today his eyes appeared more green than gray. The color reminded her of the moors after a heavy rain. He angled his ebony head, the longish hair so black that it almost held a blue tone. "My lady, Miss Cora. Miss Elana."

To her astonishment, her daughters mimicked their Aunt Berget and dipped into passably decent curtsies. Perhaps mimicking shouldn't be discouraged after all.

One impressive eyebrow rose, a distinct glint of amusement. But there was, perhaps, a challenge in his gaze. "Ah, I see ye took my advice to heart about teachin' the lasses proper comportment."

THREE

Keane almost choked on the laugh he swallowed, but mirth continued to burble behind his breastbone. Bad of him to provoke Marjorie Kennedy before she'd even set foot inside his ancestral home.

Her soft, red lips pressed into a disapproving line while sparks flew from her turbulent treacle-brown eyes. Keane would wager his new basket-hilted broadsword that she'd have the last word on the matter. Perverse as it was, he looked forward to their verbal sparring.

It was oddly invigorating, and the merest iota tantalizing.

As everyone entered the keep, he exchanged banal pleasantries with Graeme and Camden. Despite the Kennedys' genial overture last summer, a residue of strain remained between the two clans.

However, that didn't mean he didn't intend to uphold his part in mending the rift.

Neither he nor his cousins were responsible for the inciting incident, and the characters playing a role in that debacle had departed the earth years ago. It was past time to let bygones be bygones and forge a future together.

Allies were invaluable in the Highlands, and the clans had been joined by marriage decades ago—an ill-fated and unfortunate union, to be sure. Still, it made sense for the Kennedys and Buchannans to support each other.

He'd planned a hunting party for tomorrow, a bonfire for the villagers and tenants on the last day of December, and several other activities to keep his guests entertained.

Keane intended to visit a few households for first footing. Given that he matched the description of the ideal guest to cross the threshold first, much anticipation preceded his annual visits. Also, chatter and wagering commenced amongst his people regarding which fortunate households Keane would grace.

Of its own volition, his attention strayed to Marjorie Kennedy. As a red-haired woman, she epitomized the worst visitor one could entertain for first footing. Not that he believed such superstitions, but many of his people did.

Broad of shoulder and built like bulls, the Kennedy brothers studied the entry with appraising gazes. Known far and wide as expert stalkers, they ought to enjoy the hunt. Given the large numbers of people Keane anticipated feeding this week, a stag or two or three wouldn't go amiss.

Too bad wild boars no longer roamed the woodlands. He'd ordered a hog and steer butchered as well. That meat, in addition to the myriad of fowl and fish always served at such fetes, assured no one would go hungry.

"Have Bethea and Branwen returned from the village yet, Nevin?" Keane's wards, the Glanville sisters, had insisted they must have new gowns for Hogmanay, and they'd ventured to the village to collect their masterpieces today. Since they seldom asked him for anything frivolous, Keane had yielded to their pretty requests.

"Nae yet, Yer Grace," Nevin replied as he accepted the Kennedys' outward attire.

Keane's wards were taking advantage of their day out, it seemed.

In truth, Branwen had been his father's goddaughter. When the sisters' parents had died fifteen years ago, Gordan Buchannan, fifth Duke of Roxdale, became their guardian. When he'd cast off his mortal coil a mere five years later from the ague, Keane had assumed their guardianship.

Branwen and Bethea were as close as sisters to him, and he protected them as if they were. No fewer than four armed clansmen and two maids had accompanied the lasses on their outing today.

In truth, Bethea, at one and twenty, and Branwen, at twenty, ought to be married by now. Except he didn't consider any man deserving of them, and he'd restricted their social interactions for fear of something untoward happening to them as it had happened to his unfortunate mother.

Neither was pleased to be unwed, and both regularly suggested they'd end up spinsters because of him.

"As soon as they arrive home, please inform them I wish a word with them," Keane said to the servant, whose arms were laden with the Kennedys' outerwear.

He must warn Bethea and Branwen to be on their guards this week. With the number of visitors, strangers, and friends alike descending upon the keep, extra diligence was necessary.

"Indeed, Yer Grace," came the butler's muffled reply.

Berget Kennedy gave Keane a friendly glance, an openness in her features not present in the others. "I enjoyed Branwen and Bethea's company at the *cèilidh*. I quite look forward to seein' them again."

"They've anticipated yer visit, as well." He included Marjorie in his remark, but she was attending to divesting her bundled daughters of their outer garments and didn't notice. She was an attentive, gentle mother, and she quite obviously adored her children.

Keane had never experienced a mother's love. Well, not that he could remember, in any event.

No one had ever mentioned whether his mother had loved him. Until now, he'd never been curious about what he'd missed, but something in Marjorie's demeanor caused a queer pull he couldn't describe.

As soon as the lasses had removed their outerwear, he escorted the Kennedy entourage into the great hall and, with a casual flick of his hand, called for refreshments. As he'd directed prior to the Kennedys' arrival, bathwater warmed in the kitchens for them. A pair of maids scurried from the hall: one to oversee the food and drink and the other the baths, no doubt.

He had yet to glance in Marjorie's direction again, mindful that showing too much attention could easily be misinterpreted by those present. Chatter that his interest in the beautiful widow was more than simple courtesy was something he didn't want started.

Nonetheless, he felt the daggers she glared at him as surely as if she hurled the blades at his chest. Obviously, she'd not forgiven him for reprimanding her daughters, or for refusing to dance with her last August.

She hadn't any way of knowing he seldom danced, and that he wasn't rebuffing her when he'd not asked her. Something so nonsensical as her rejection shouldn't sting, and yet it did.

Still, he admitted to himself, he had been an insufferably rude bastard. But he hoped they wouldn't be at cross purposes her entire visit. Scraping another approving glance over her fine-boned face and delectable figure, he reconsidered his initial appraisal. Mayhap, his bold admiration of her womanly assets a few minutes ago had prompted her current pique.

In truth, there was something about the widow that drew him unlike any other woman, and it intrigued as much as disturbed him. From the moment he'd met Marjorie Kennedy, instinct had warned Keane to tread carefully. But last summer, he'd stupidly allowed whatever the enigmatic force was to mesmerize him those first few minutes they'd eaten together.

Once again, as he had been dozens of times these past months, he was transported to Killeaggian last August.

Keane had glanced around, taking in the stunning redhead and her lasses. She had smiled and chatted animatedly beside him as her daughters sat across the table, their mouths stuffed to overflowing.

Sitting there, the four of them, they'd looked like a happy family.

Odin's toes. A family.

The notion had utterly terrified him, far worse than the hand-to-hand combats he'd fought.

When the two lasses' antics had escalated to the point that they had spewed crumbs onto the table, he'd seized the opportunity to break the discomfiting atmosphere by condemning their behavior. He'd been out of line and had gone beyond the mark.

A first for him—scolding someone else's children.

And now, the alluring Englishwoman with hair the shade of sunset was in his home, and, by God, the atmosphere felt dangerously similar to that of last August.

What was this scintillating, potent current between him and Marjorie Kennedy?

Did she feel it too?

He couldn't discern if her avoidance of his gaze was

because she was still miffed or if she was similarly disturbed by his presence.

Hands resting on his hips, Keane scanned the assembled crowd of perhaps two score and assured himself all was well. Their numbers would double by tomorrow evening and swell even further as the villagers and his tenants joined the Hogmanay celebration.

He hadn't entertained on this scale before.

This gathering was part of a calculated plan to change the perception of the Roxdale duchy—a long overdue and disregarded necessity. Whereas the previous generations of dukes had been self-serving, demanding, harsh, and cared little about those they were responsible for, Keane strove to change that perception to one of fairness and benevolence.

Sending another circumspect glance around the hall, he nodded to himself, satisfied. Aye, this was a good start. Well-fed and most nursing a cup of ale or a glass of wine, his guests sat or stood in clusters discussing whatever inanity people found to babble about at such functions.

Trentwick's interior wasn't gaudy or ornate. Nonetheless, the castle was magnificent in its own right. A hearty fire burned in the hearth large enough to accommodate five average-sized men within its immense spans. The flames cast cavorting shadows on those huddled nearby absorbing the hearth's warmth.

Pennants and weaponry adorned three of the stone walls, as did various garlands of greeneries. Clean, hospitable, and welcoming. Exactly as Keane had ordered, and his servants hadn't failed his expectations.

A swell of pride engulfed him. Despite his lineage consisting mainly of monumental arses—the prior dukes, that was—they'd maintained the keep and grounds to a standard even he couldn't fault.

The coffers and grain houses overflowed. The fields, barns, and stables were full.

It seemed the only areas his forefathers had lacked mastery in were kindness and benevolence. *And morals.* Don't forget that. His forefathers had rutted liked wild animals, drunk like pished tipplers, and, to his knowledge, not a one had been faithful to his duchess.

Even his esteemed sire had brazenly kept his mistress at Trentwick for a couple of years. She'd run off with one of his guards when Keane had been eleven or twelve. After she'd caught him, yet again, tupping another maid.

Given the prior dukes' penchants for swiving anything in a skirt, he wouldn't be surprised if he weren't related to half of the villagers and tenants. Odd that the fifth duke had never remarried or produced additional offspring, legitimate or otherwise. Particularly considering the resentment he harbored toward Keane.

Could the few months of marriage to his mother have truly put him off matrimony so very much?

Half a year. Six months.

That had been the extent of his parents' union. His mother had been well into her fourth month of increasing before the forced ceremony had taken place, and she'd died weeks after Keane's birth.

So many questions plagued him.

Questions that would forever remain unanswered.

Keane's attention snared on a group of Highlanders loudly chortling and slapping one another's backs a few feet from the fireplace.

Bothan and Lorne.

Displeasure skewed Keane's brows into a harsh vee. No bloody surprise his uncle and cousin were amongst the rowdier attendees. They'd revel to excess the entire time, and past experience dictated any females below fifty years of age weren't safe from their groping or vulgar insinuations.

Uncle Bothan Buchannan and his son had been amongst the first arrivals. In point of fact, they hadn't been invited but had somehow learned of the gathering. Brazen as hell and despite the lack of invitation, a missive arrived a fortnight ago stating their intentions to attend. Given they took after their unsavory Buchannan predecessors, Keane would've preferred they'd not.

In truth, he'd rather not acknowledge the kinship at all.

His scowl deepened as Lorne made a ribald comment of some sort and palmed his groin in a crude imitation of sexual congress. *Odin's teeth!* There were innocent women and children present. So help him God, he hadn't a qualm about sending one or both on their way at the slightest provocation.

A rift between Gordan Buchannan and his twin had spared Keane his uncle's company for most of his youth. However, when Gordan's health began failing, first Bothan, then his irritating son, had put in regular, unsolicited appearances at Trentwick.

Not that Gordan agreed to see them.

He'd ordered his twin and nephew from the keep each time with the threat of bodily harm should they return. They did, of course—came slithering back, speculative glints in their greedy eyes.

As was his implacable, unforgiving nature, Gordan had remained mulishly obstinate until he drew his last quavering breath, a proclivity which had infuriated Bothan and Lorne alike. Keane had never learned the cause of the dispute between Gordan and Bothan, and his uncle adamantly refused to discuss the reason for the quarrel.

So many, many dark secrets haunted the Buchannans. If Keane were the superstitious sort, he might believe the whispers about a family curse. One irrefutable truth remained, however: if he never saw his uncle or cousin again, he'd not grieve the loss.

Ever vigilant, he slid a glance around the room, taking in his guests and servants.

He'd directed his female staff to keep their distance from Bothan and Lorne and to work in pairs. He'd also instructed the menservants to be extra diligent to protect the women in Keane's employ.

His uncle and cousin had reputations for forcing their attentions on unwilling lasses and, by God, during this stay, no woman would fear for her virtue. This visit, Keane had gone so far as to assign them isolated chambers away from the other guests' and servants' quarters.

His focus lingered on three maids chatting near the hearth before gravitating to a pair of forest green and black liveried footmen roaming the room dispersing beverages and collecting empty cups. The Hogmanay celebration hadn't been a secret, but he suspected one of his servants regularly passed information to his father's twin.

Keane expected loyalty from his servants, clan, and tenants, and it was past time he learned the conspirator's identity and dismissed the traitor. The notion that someone conveyed information to his uncle had been in the back of his mind for months, but he couldn't conceive which of his servants had betrayed his trust.

Bothan and Lorne always seemed mysteriously abreast of everything that occurred at Trentwick. On more than one occasion, Keane had to remind his opinionated uncle that *he* wasn't the duke.

That truth always earned a thunderous scowl and a muttered curse.

In truth, Bothan and Lorne held Keane in no fonder

esteem than he did them. Yet, here they were, like pests or vermin. Always appearing when one least desired them to make their presence known, and never disappearing as quickly as one would prefer.

Hands and jaw clenched, he speared his sot of a cousin a lethal glare.

At this very moment, Lorne all but leered at Marjorie as if she were a dockside strumpet. He licked his lips, his focus dropping to the teasing swell of her breasts.

Keane took an involuntary step forward, prepared to throttle the wretch. A broken nose ought to knock the lecherous glint from his eyes.

Then—blast his bloody plan—he recalled his purpose in inviting everyone for the Hogmanay festivities. He would be no better than Lorne or the other generations of Buchannans before him if he planted his fist in his cousin's lascivious face, *damn it all*.

Features schooled into an indecipherable mask, Keane permitted himself a long blink. God's teeth, but it would be magnificently satisfying to feel the bones of Lorne's prominent nose flatten beneath his blow. He wanted to challenge any man who looked upon Marjorie with anything other than brotherly interest, but he couldn't very well fight with half the men present and still claim he was a better man than his predecessors.

And, in truth, he *wasn't* any better than the other men.

He, too, had taken in the curves a man typically marked and appreciated.

Marjorie's deep blue gown emphasized her small waist and bountiful bosom. The rich velvet also enhanced her vibrant gold-and-bronze-threaded red hair, winsomely mussed from her extended journey. Her creamy skin glowed pearly white, and her eyes, the color of freshly brewed coffee, were rich and warm and delicious.

Nae, her eyes arena delicious, ye cabbage head.

Aye, but those full berry-red lips are.

Her daughters clung to her hands, their bright blue eyes wide with apprehension and curiosity. Every now and again, one slid him a fretful glance, and shame lanced him. He'd been an utter arse to the wee lassies.

The impish things *he'd* done as a lad had driven his long-suffering nurse and then his less-patient tutors half-mad. Keane had been up to his chin in mischief and misadventures at their age. He'd overstepped by chastising them. At the convicting memory, he plowed a hand through his hair.

Lorne still openly gawped at Marjorie, sizing up her feminine attributes, and Keane gritted his teeth. His cousin best keep his lewd attentions to himself, by damn. No Buchannan —not Keane, not Bothan, and assuredly not Lorne—would ever give another Kennedy woman cause for distress.

At least not while under his roof.

For her part, Marjorie was either unaware of Lorne's ogling or a master at ignoring unwanted scrutiny. Not once did she make eye contact with him, and her face remained a mask of benign serenity.

Keane knew full well the fiery siren her outwardly calm mien disguised. Hadn't he been on the receiving end of her wrath? She'd been nothing short of magnificent: eyes flashing fury-laden sparks, breasts heaving, her breath coming in short, raspy pants.

Och, aye. Magnificent indeed.

A grin almost tipped his mouth at the descriptive, oh-so-polite way she'd told him to shove his head up his arse in her modulated British accent. So prim and proper sounding as she very improperly insulted him.

At the time, he hadn't found her ire amusing, but, in the months since, the memory never failed to summon a grin or chuckle. By damn, Marjorie Kennedy had spirit. Spirit she tried to hide behind a demure façade. But he was on to her charade, and he quite anticipated scaling her battlements and ramparts.

Moreover, he quite anticipated discovering what treasures lay within.

Keane snorted. He was a damn, bloody fool for even considering doing so because he'd have to woo and court her. And he strongly suspected, she'd try to scratch his eyes out if he did. Until she, like his Scottish wildcats, realized he meant her no harm and tamed the wild creature within her.

FOUR

Across the hall, a group of Highlanders acknowledged the Kennedy brothers' entrance with friendly nods. *Och, aye.* The McPhersons were related to the MacKays, and Liam MacKay was a particular friend of Graeme's.

"Please excuse my lady and me," Graeme said with an apologetic quirk of his mouth. "Bryston McPherson hasna met my bride yet."

His great hulk of a cousin had taken to married life with enthusiasm. Keane wouldn't have believed it had he not witnessed the transformation himself. With a slight dip of his head, he acknowledged his cousin's request. "By all means."

These gatherings always reunited kin and kith. Most of the clans could claim an affinity with one another due to a marriage at one time. In fact, the branches of family trees were often so entwined it became difficult to detect which branch belonged to which clan. As he well knew, however, such unions didn't guarantee peace and accord between the tribes.

"Excuse me, I have a matter I wish to discuss with Bryston too," Camden said a trifle too casually.

Keane could hazard a guess what that conversation

entailed. It assuredly wouldn't take place in Lady Kennedy's presence, however. Bryston McPherson, a former privateer, and Camden had questionable business dealings not always sanctioned by the Crown. Namely, smuggling.

Although, Keane suspected that a few of their activities were, in fact, merely a cover for covert directives from His Majesty. Should they be discovered, the king would naturally disavow any knowledge of their escapades.

George I had approached Keane with a similar proposition. A request which Keane had politely but firmly declined. If he hadn't been bent on restoring the duchy's reputation, or if he'd had a brother or two to inherit lest calamity befall him while in service to His Majesty, he'd have accepted. But he hadn't any brothers, nor an heir, and there was no way in Hades he would permit his uncle or cousin to inherit the dukedom.

He'd seen the neglected condition of his uncle's estate, the suffering of his tenants, and the fear, contempt, and distrust of those in his employ.

"I'm sure you do," Keane drawled, giving his cousin a knowing look.

Camden grinned and, after patting his nieces upon their bright, gingery heads, followed his brother.

In an instant, Marjorie and her daughters stood alone. Rather bereft and forlorn, in truth.

Forgotten?

How often did that happen?

From the carefully passive look on her face and the slightly hurt and uneasy gleam in her pretty eyes, it happened often enough that she'd learned to conceal her distress.

Alone in a foreign country in a household of people she didn't know.

Much like his mother, except Mother, at least, had been a Scot.

He may not have ever known his mother, but what he'd heard of her bore the makings of a Shakespearian tragedy. She'd been despoiled—forced to marry a man she didn't know and had no desire to wed. Afterward, a vengeful Gordan Buchannan had ignored and disdained her. Frail and home-sick, and utterly unhappy, his mother had died at the tender age of eighteen, a mere month after Keane's birth.

To this day, the ugly whispers he'd heard of his pathetic mother's suffering rested like a festering glob in his gut.

His father had done nothing to make a difficult situation tolerable, either.

Pulling on his earlobe, he surreptitiously observed Marjorie.

How long had she lived in Scotland anyway?

Why hadn't she returned to England when Sion died?

"Your home is magnificent, Your Grace. I'm sure there's a great deal of history attached to the keep." And there she went, making polite conversation to fill the yawning gap caused by the other Kennedys deserting her mere minutes after their arrival.

Did she always do what was polite and expected?

Lorne and Bothan excused themselves from the Highlanders they'd been conversing with. Faces wreathed in too bright smiles and their boot heels clacking noisily on the stone floor, they shoved and elbowed a path to Keane.

Eager for an introduction, were they?

Keane was of half a mind to take Marjorie by the arm and lead her from the room. Instead, he reflexively fisted his hands at the distinct male interest Lorne levied at Marjorie from his bulgy, thickly hooded eyes.

Thank God, Keane hadn't inherited that particular Buchannan trait.

For her part, Marjorie's attention remained on her surprisingly well-behaved daughters. After Keane's first encounter with the lasses, he'd suspected they were indulged and cosseted. Spoiled by their mother, perhaps out of a misplaced sense of guilt that they were fatherless.

Observing the docile lasses, their eyes wide and inquisitive as they examined the hall, he furrowed his brow slightly. He might've jumped to an unwarranted conclusion, and a stab of guilt at his hasty judgment pricked him.

The girls before him were not impudent, ill-behaved imps.

He observed Marjorie as she took in the great hall, offering a reserved smile now and again. How could he not admire her poise? Her self-possession?

When he'd stepped from the keep and seen her, face upturned and breasts pointing skyward, awe had fleetingly overcome him. And he, Keane Evan Sloan Buchannan, sixth Duke of Roxdale, did not awe easily. In truth, he didn't give place to worthless emotion or sentiment. Hence his momentary lapse when he'd first seen her outside his keep had proved all the more disconcerting.

True, he'd believed her attractive at Killeaggian Tower last August. Her mass of brilliant red hair, reflecting bronze and copper and every hue of the sunset, held him in thrall. Though red-haired women were supposed to be bad luck, *her* brilliant hair made the risk worthwhile.

Tall and slender, she possessed gently rounded curves in all the places a man yearned to smooth his palm over and trail his lips across. Satiny warm, soft places. Places that held delicious secrets, tantalizing sensations, and delectable promises. Her thick-lashed eyes, a shade between treacle and rich whisky, revealed kindness but also suffering.

She was attractive in an unaffected way. But when she smiled—God help him. Her smile transformed her into a blinding, mesmerizing beauty. When he'd seen her in the courtyard, her silky lashes fanning her creamy cheeks and her face a picture of serenity as snowflakes swirled around her, he'd been struck dumb.

She'd been like a fairy princess or an ethereal being.

Then she opened her eyelids and her magnificent gaze had tangled with his. And for several interminable heartbeats, something powerful and undefinable had traveled between them.

At last, his common sense had returned, slamming him back to reality, and Keane had deliberately skewed his mouth in a sardonic manner certain to put her on her guard.

Never again would a Kennedy accuse a Buchannan of unwanted or untoward attentions.

Even after Keane's birth, and until his dying day, the former duke had privately vowed he wasn't Keane's father. As his mother had died when he was scarcely a month old, he'd never known the truth of his conception.

However, the man the world considered his father could scarcely stand to look upon him. When Gordan Buchannan, fifth Duke of Roxdale, breathed his last, Keane had grieved for what had never been and what could never be, not for the man's death. A bitter, unforgiving curmudgeon who wouldn't even permit Keane to call him father but demanded he address him as *Yer Grace*, so great had been his rancor toward his heir.

A niggling suspicion had always plagued Keane. A perpetual doubt he'd never voiced.

Why would Gordan continue to avow his innocence?

Even after his wife had given him a son and heir?

Honor? Pride?

Perhaps. But *perhaps* it was something more.

"Keane, son, must we introduce ourselves to yer guests?" Uncle Bothan chided, his grizzled eyebrows contorting high on his prominent forehead.

"No' at all, Uncle." Necessity required Keane to introduce his uncle and cousin. Stifling his annoyance and reluctance, he did so as succinctly as possible.

"My lady," Lorne said, bowing low over the hand Marjorie dutifully extended. "I'd be honored if ye'd agree to dance with me after dinner."

Marjorie's practiced smile didn't falter, but nor did it light her magnificent eyes. She smoothly withdrew her hand and promptly gathered her daughters near. "I regret I cannot make such a promise, Mr. Buchannan. I do not know how long it will take for my daughters to settle this evening, and I shall not leave them if they're ill-at-ease."

She flashed Keane a swift glance, a spark of defiance in her eyes.

Ah, she'd meant that as a warning for him as well.

He hadn't taken her for one to hold a grudge. But then they'd only met once before, and neither had been on their best behavior.

"Perfectly understandable," Keane agreed with forced cheer and a jaunty smile, mainly to irk Lorne.

As expected, his cousin dredged up a disapproving scowl, his mouth turned downward into a sullen pout. Such petulance from a grown man was nauseating. He behaved like a coddled child denied a sweetmeat.

"Please feel free to request a tray if ye feel the need," Keane told Marjorie, redoubling his efforts to peeve his peeved cousin. "Though, of course, we'll miss yer company as we sup."

Astonishment and perhaps a little gratitude riddled the

look she cut him from beneath ginger-tipped lashes. He'd managed to surprise her.

"Och, well, she canna remain in the nursery the entire week," Uncle Bothan insisted. He winked, his sly gaze sliding between her and Lorne. "My son wishes to further yer acquaintance, my lady."

And what Lorne wanted he generally took. Without regard to what anyone else might desire.

Alarm flickered in Marjorie's eyes, and she practically shrank into herself.

A violent urge to protect her had Keane stepping forward and offering his arm. "Permit me to escort ye to yer chamber."

Something akin to a jealous growl escaped Lorne before Uncle leveled him a quelling glare and slapped him upon his back. "I could use a wee dram. How about ye, Son?"

As if they hadn't indulged in several not-so-wee tots already, as their slightly bloodshot eyes attested.

Lorne grumbled his acquiescence before spearing Keane with a rancorous scowl and marching off with his sire, all starch and stiff-legged offense. Two years older than Keane, Lorne often behaved like a recalcitrant pup—a trait wholly unbecoming in a grown man.

"My lady?" Keane indicated his extended elbow.

Her gaze flicked from his arm to his face and back to his arm. Would she refuse him? The slim column of her throat worked as she swallowed. "That's not necessary, Your Grace," Marjorie demurred, no artifice in her tone.

He liked her voice. Though she spoke with an English accent, her voice held a husky undertone. Rather than putting one off, the tenor invited a man in, tempted him to explore the uniqueness that was Marjorie Kennedy.

God's ballocks.

Was he, Keane, Duke of Roxdale, truly waxing poetic over

a woman he scarcely knew? A woman who'd intruded upon his thoughts too many times to count these past months?

When she still resisted taking his arm, he quirked an eyebrow in mock offense, amused at her show of defiance.

"Though I truly appreciate the gesture," she rushed to assure him.

Och, so she'd detected his true motives.

Why was she so eager to pacify him now when, four months ago, she'd told him quite succinctly what she thought of him. But then, she had been defending her daughters. Hmm, it seemed she wouldn't protect herself, but God help him or anyone else who trifled with the tigress's children.

Such fierce, maternal protectiveness caused an irregular stirring within him.

"'Tis nae token gesture but a sincere offer," he countered, low and gentle as if calming a skittish mare.

Such skepticism crinkled her forehead that he would've chuckled had he not been convinced she'd take offense. And for reasons Keane would rather not examine too closely, offending Marjorie Kennedy was the last thing he wanted to do.

"You have guests to attend," she put forth, sweeping an astute gaze around the hall.

In that one swift perusal, he'd warrant she took in everything occurring in the hall, including the maid flirting with a footman by the window, and Lady Constance Abercrombie hiding a bored yawn behind her hand as she sat beside her dozing spinster aunt.

Wait. What is she doing here?

His attention veered back to her.

When had she arrived, and where were her father and brother?

Ballocks.

Had she come without them?

He nearly swore aloud and rolled his eyes. Lady Constance had only ever been included because Keane wanted to purchase the acreage they owned adjacent to Trentwick. In point of fact, the Abercrombies' presence at Trentwick functions was solely due to that desire. Keane couldn't very well invite the rest of her family and ask that she not attend, which was his preference.

If ever a woman had marriage on her mind, it was Lady Constance Abercrombie. From the hints repeatedly sent his way by her doddering father, he'd include the lands Keane wanted in her marital settlement. Bruce Abercrombie, Earl of Newville, had implied many, *many* times how very much he'd appreciate a duke as a son-in-law.

A raven-haired beauty with violet eyes, impeccable manners, and a lineage royalty might envy, Lady Constance epitomized everything the world believed a duchess ought to exemplify.

Except Keane had witnessed her true colors.

She pinched the female servants, kicked his cats, complained if her bread wasn't sliced a precise thickness, criticized everything from the temperature of her bathwater to the strength of her tea, mocked those less fortunate, and in all things acted superior and condescending.

In short, Lady Constance Abercrombie was a shrewish bitch.

He'd never take such a petty, contrary woman to wife. Not even to acquire the fertile lands ideal for his tenants to grow barley and oats.

Lady Constance caught him looking in her direction and regally inclined her head while not so subtly brushing her hand across the ample expanse of flesh visible above her bodice. On numerous occasions, she'd shamelessly invited him to partake of her charms.

Which, of course, meant a direct march to the kirk afterward.

Did she truly think all men were governed by their cock?

Och, aye. Most are, he was obliged to admit.

"And I don't wish to be an inconvenience." Marjorie's soft objection brought him back to the present and the bonnie woman standing rather forlornly beside him. She didn't defy him outright but used practiced diplomacy to extricate herself.

Without acknowledging Lady Constance's blatant invitation, Keane turned his full regard to the Englishwoman and her daughters. He could feel Lady Constance's incensed glare boring into his back. Two furious, scorching arrows. He'd taken to treating her coldly to discourage her interest, but to no avail. He'd admire her tenaciousness if her goal weren't to snare him.

What had Marjorie said?

I dinna wish to be an inconvenience.

He'd vow Marjorie lived by that motto.

Dinna mind me. I'll make do.

From his brief encounters with her, he'd come to a few conclusions. She made no demands, had no expectations of her brothers-in-law, and essentially tried to make herself invisible.

Except Marjorie Kennedy was a brilliant, sparkling star. Fiery and bright, brilliant and remarkable, and impossible to overlook. Unless a man was blind or dead. *Or...* An unbidden thought interrupted his contemplations. Unless that man regarded her as a sister. He scraped a swift look in the direction of the Kennedys talking earnestly with Bryston.

That realization shouldn't have produced the satisfaction it did.

"Mama?" The youngest lass pointed a wee finger to the entrance.

Her daughters had remained so quiet and obedient that he'd almost forgotten their presence.

Ah, I see ye took my advice about teaching them proper comportment.

These lasses' polite behavior stemmed from years of instruction and practice. Something akin to shame clawed Keane's conscience for his contemptuous remark earlier.

Christ on the blessed cross. I'm a bloody cod pated arse.

"What *are* they?" Cora whispered, her voice a combination of fascination and fear.

Marjorie turned to look to where her daughter pointed.

"Giant kitties." Elana gasped and surged forward, but her mother seized her arm while tossing a frantic glance over her shoulder to Keane.

Grinning, he cocked an eyebrow. "Miss Cora and Miss Elana, would ye like to meet Chimera and Sphynx?" He winked and whispered *sotto voce*, "They're Scottish wildcats I rescued as kittens."

"Are they friendly?" Looking markedly uncertain, Marjorie bit her lower lip.

Hell and damn. How he longed to suck that plump pillow into his mouth and worship the tender sweetness the way it deserved.

Clearing his throat, he tamped down his lust. *For God's sake, mon.* Her daughters stood but inches away, and he lusted after Marjorie as if he were a callow youth.

"I'm not sure..." Again, she sent him a questioning glance.

He couldn't fault her for her caution. He'd already learned she'd take on anyone and anything to safeguard her daughters.

"Aye, quite gentle." He winked once more. For her, this time.

Her pretty brown eyes rounded in surprise, and fetching pink tinted her porcelain cheeks.

The cats sat on their haunches, their keen citrine eyes taking in the intruders to their domicile with bored disinterest. To the inexperienced eye, the rangy, thick-coated felines appeared like overgrown tabbies. *Immensely* overgrown tabby cats.

Chimera caught sight of the lasses first. Ears twitching, she nonchalantly padded across the floor, her long tail swishing lazily in her wake. Several guests warily eyed the lithe feline. Four feet from the tips of their black noses to the tips of their bushy ebony tails, the cats frequently gave newcomers quite a start the first time they saw them.

Not to be outdone by her sister, Sphynx yawned, exposing impressive canines before she too sauntered toward the girls.

Her distrustful gaze trained on the feline sisters, Marjorie emitted a little worried sound in her throat and drew her daughters closer.

Keane stepped forward and touched her arm. "I've raised them since before their eyes opened. I give ye my word, Marjorie, they're gentle as kittens."

He was mindful not to say harmless, for he'd seen what they could do if angered.

A former stable hand had despised cats and, unbeknownst to Keane, teased and taunted the pair unmercifully. One day, Chimera had had enough and pinned the scunner to the floor, her mouth upon his throat but not breaking the skin. Had she wished to do so, she could have ended his life in an instant.

He'd fled that day and never returned. Good thing too, because Keane would've dismissed him after giving him a well-deserved thrashing.

Eyes half-shut, the cats rubbed their heads against Keane's calves, marking their territory. He squatted and scratched behind their ears. "Ye want to meet the lassies, do ye?" He brushed a hand over each of their big heads. "Sit."

One of the few tricks he'd taught them.

Both promptly sat, gazing at him expectantly, yet looking appropriately bored and put upon as cats were wont to do. The cats hissed every time Lady Constance, Uncle Bothan, or Lorne came near.

Smart animals. They knew offal when they saw it.

He held out a hand to Elana. "Come here. 'Tis all right, I promise ye."

After sending her mother a questioning glance and receiving a tentative nod, she took Keane's hand. He drew her forward. "This lovely lass is Chimera. She's slightly bigger than her sister, just as ye are bigger than yer sister."

Eyes gleaming, Elana grinned at him and then at Cora. "What's the other one's name?"

"She's Sphynx," he said. "Let them smell ye."

Elana remained perfectly still as Chimera and Sphynx nosed her. Then, to his astonishment, Chimera pressed her head into Elana's belly and began purring. Loudly.

"She likes ye," he whispered. While not unfriendly with people they knew, the over-sized cats generally avoided strangers.

"May I pet her, Yer Grace?" Elana whispered back. "Pleeeease?"

She extended the word into a plea, her blue eyes wide in earnest supplication.

Nodding, he slanted his head to watch Sphynx. She'd wandered to Cora and similarly sniffed the lass and then her mother. As if to outdo her sister, she lay upon her back. Belly and paws upward, and making little chirping noises, she invited the small girl to rub her belly.

With a delighted giggle, Cora was only too happy to oblige.

Soon throaty purrs echoed around them.

Cupping his nape, he chuckled. "Och, that's a first."

Keane glanced up and caught Marjorie regarding him, confusion shadowing her fine-boned features. Arching an eyebrow, he silently challenged.

What now?

The graceful curve of her rosy mouth softened into an astonished half-smile. "Why, you're not a cold-hearted brute at all."

FIVE

Four hours later, Marjorie hummed and tapped her toes in time to the lively reel as she watched laughing couples, many sweating profusely, gaily sway, dip, and turn in time to the lilting music. For certain, the Highlanders relished dancing almost as much as their whisky.

She'd originally intended to eat with her daughters, tell them a story, then bathe and seek her bed early. After all, her purpose for attending was to show support for the Kennedys, and she needn't join the others for dinner and the dancing afterward to do so.

Nor did she have any desire to witness couples flirting and engaging in courtship when she'd put all such notions from her mind. And rightly so. She had daughters to raise, and that —*only that*—should remain her focus.

Not her loneliness or the peculiar unrest that plagued her of late.

However, Cora and Elana had other plans after their supper and baths. Plans which included oversized, purring cats indolently splayed alongside them. Beside themselves with excitement, her daughters had pleaded for Sphynx and Chimera to sleep atop their beds.

Marjorie still wasn't wholly comfortable with the large felines weighing as much as Cora lurking about her daughters. However, the cheery, plump-cheeked maid, Phemie, assigned to the nursery during the house party, assured her she'd watch the girls like hawks.

Phemie vowed the cats were so mild-mannered and tame that they didn't even hunt mice.

Marjorie strongly doubted that assertion. Somewhat reluctantly, she'd kissed her daughters' soft, sweet, soap-scented cheeks and, after prayers and a dutiful pat atop each loudly purring cat's slightly rough head, bid the lasses a goodnight.

Much refreshed and finally warm after a lavender and rosemary-scented soak, she wore one of her favorite gowns. A satin and velvet fern-green creation trimmed with gold. With her hair piled high on her head except for a few long curls trailing over her left shoulder, she didn't feel quite so out of place. The only jewelry she owned, simple emerald earrings and a matching pendant, completed her ensemble.

A glance out her bedchamber window revealed the snowfall had stopped and only three or four inches blanketed the ground. Unless it began again, she needn't worry about being snowed in after all, and her host's plans for the week would remain unthwarted by petulant weather.

Why that mattered to her, she couldn't hazard a guess.

Well, that wasn't particularly true. If Keane were otherwise engaged, she'd not have to bear his company.

Would that be so very bad?

Earlier today, she'd have adamantly said yes. But after his astonishing behavior when introducing his cats to her daughters, she'd reassessed Keane, Duke of Roxdale. Mayhap he truly wasn't such a brute, and that tingle of pleasure she'd first experienced when she'd seen him at Killeaggian Tower flitted around her middle again.

Or was it her heart?

Such thoughts were nonsensical flimflam.

Inhaling deeply, Marjorie gave herself a mental shake. She was here as an emissary of the Kennedy clan. Nothing more. With dogged determination, she ordered her wandering mind back to the present.

Dinner had passed pleasantly enough, as long as she avoided looking in Lorne Buchannan's direction, who sat several seats farther along the table. Praise God and all the saints for that. The food was sumptuous and excellently prepared, though her appetite had increasingly diminished as the meal progressed and Keane's cousin continued to pay her marked attention.

His lecherous perusal caused her nape hair to stand on end, and she'd nearly excused herself to collect a wrap to protect her already modest neckline from his probing stare.

Keane might've angered her, and he certainly unnerved her, but he'd never made her want to flee his presence. Every time Lorne turned his oily gaze to her, she yearned to scrub her skin until it was raw and then hide in a wardrobe or under a bed.

From the moment Lorne Kennedy had laid eyes upon her, she'd felt him undressing her. He regarded her with ill-concealed lust, and she couldn't believe no one had noticed. Never before had a man made her feel so uncomfortable simply by looking at her, openly stripping her naked with his licentious gaze.

She could've hugged Keane when he'd rescued her earlier, saving her from Lorne and his father's insistence that she become *acquainted* with Lorne. She knew exactly what kind of acquaintance the rotter desired.

In truth, the duke might've noticed the disturbing glint in his cousin's insipid brown eyes.

Flicking her fan open, Marjorie smiled as Berget and Graeme swept past and then hid a grin behind her fan as Camden followed a few steps later, partnered by none other than Bethea Glanville. A rather intimidating man with a scarred face, his long hair secured in a knot at the back of his head and several tattoos visible on his ringed fingers, led her sister, Branwen, through the steps.

Bryston McPherson, she presumed, though Graeme hadn't introduced her to the Scot either. That truth seemed to have slipped his and Camden's minds when they'd rushed off to greet him. In point of fact, they'd not thought to introduce her to anyone, and she wasn't sure whether to be vexed or amused.

Oh, they didn't mean to be unkind or neglectful, and she didn't harbor a doubt they'd suffer chagrin at their oversight when it dawned on them. *If* it ever did.

Were all brothers so neglectful?

She hadn't any brothers other than the Kennedys.

She took in the dancers promenading down the line. Neither Granville miss looked entirely pleased, yet each kept their pretty gray gazes trained on their partners as the big Scots guided them among the other revelers.

Camden and Bryston McPherson, however, appeared anything but disinterested.

Well now, that might prove very interesting.

Very, *very* interesting indeed.

Keane had done well with his wards. The thought came unbidden, and it surprised her she'd found another thing to admire about him. She'd been so determined to see his faults that acknowledging he wasn't a complete bounder caused a little skip of gladness.

He'd taken on the role of guardian—*what?*—a decade ago? Perchance slightly longer? In truth, she wasn't certain, as she'd been a new bride in a new country and Sion hadn't spoken of his estranged cousin much.

A stunning, ebony-haired beauty, sumptuous in violet and black, paraded past on the arm of a strikingly handsome gentleman—the kind of man who made maidens gasp in awed wonder.

Marjorie, however, wasn't an inexperienced, impressionable schoolgirl.

Besides, the man clearly only had eyes for the woman by his side. Marjorie gave a little smile at how he stared with such adoration.

Sion used to look at her like that.

With a start, she realized the beauty stared directly at her, pure venom in the woman's narrowed-eyed gaze.

At the blatant animosity, Marjorie's smile withered.

Who was she, and why the unprovoked malice?

It was unnerving to have such malevolence directed at her by a stranger. Perhaps she'd ask Berget if she knew who the lady was. For certain, she'd avoid the hostile woman's company, if possible. All the more reason to sequester herself in the nursery for the bulk of the visit.

Positioned by the entry in case her daughters needed her, Marjorie absently searched the ballroom for a certain tall, raven-haired Scot. One whose presence commanded attention and who'd commandeered her thoughts since her arrival.

Prior to that too.

No small amount of truth there.

Waving her fan, she once more scrutinized the ballroom. *Pshaw.* She'd done that all evening. Found herself seeking Keane, even when she severely admonished herself not to.

Catching herself humming and swaying to the music,

Marjorie stopped and quickly looked around. No one seemed to have noticed, not even the woman who'd glared at her earlier. Laughing, the beauty now leaned close to the gentleman, batted her eyelashes, and coyly placed her hand upon his arm.

His focus trained on her ample cleavage, he smiled and, leaning down, whispered in her ear. Her smile turned sultry and inviting.

Feeling very much like a voyeur, Marjorie promptly returned her attention to the dancers. Other than her brothers-in-law, she hadn't danced with anyone since Sion's death. Not that there'd been many opportunities either. The Kennedys didn't entertain, or at least they hadn't regularly. Now that Berget had married Graeme, that would likely change.

Marjorie adored dancing.

She wasn't particularly adept, but the music captivated and carried her away. Quite simply, dancing was fun. Sion had indulged her passion for dancing and never denied her the opportunity.

A nascent smile tipped her mouth as she recalled her gentle giant of a husband. He'd been a good man, kind and generous and affectionate. She'd been fortunate to have loved and been loved in return, even if it was for too brief a period.

A distinguished-looking matron with a plethora of bright feathers adorning her high wig dipped her chin toward Marjorie. She returned Lady Kilpatrick's greeting with a warm smile. The woman moved with proud grace as if she knew her importance, and the crowd parted before her like the Red Sea before Moses.

Marjorie's smile widened a trifle for a fleeting moment.

Smiles were astonishing things. An unspoken language all their own. A simple upward sweep of one's lips might soothe hurt feelings, dissolve anger, offer sympathy, bring comfort, encourage, demonstrate approval, or show joy and happiness.

Or disguise heartbreak and sorrow.

And the recipient never knew what that bent mouth hid behind the false cheer.

"Ah, there ye are, my lovely," a man's gravely, slightly slurred voice breathed into her ear, his whisky-laden breath causing her to wrinkle her nose in distaste.

At once, she stepped away and whirled to face Lorne Buchannan. "You are presumptuous, sir."

He grinned a lop-sided drunken smirk. "I like yer spirit, lass. I've waited all evenin' to claim ye for a dance. I saw the way ye looked at me durin' our introduction and throughout supper."

"You are mistaken," she replied frostily.

He licked his fleshy lips, his focus trained on her breasts rapidly rising and falling in her agitation. He gave her a sly, disgusting wink. "Nae need to be coy. I ken yer a widow with a widow's *needs*."

What?

She blinked several times, uncertain she'd heard correctly.

Widow's needs?

He didn't mean?

Oh, the insufferable bounder!

She snapped her fan closed.

How dare he, the blackguard?

Glancing around and assuring they weren't observed, he sidled nearer and she swore her flesh recoiled in revulsion.

Her nose certainly did, for he stank, pure and simple. She'd not been close enough to smell his rank odor when Keane had introduced them this afternoon, but a sickening, musty sweet aroma wafted from his person. The stench gagged her, and she swallowed against the bile surging up the back of her throat.

"I ken a private place we can be alone, lass." He fondled his groin beneath his coat while lifting his eyebrows suggestively.

My God. Did his vileness have no boundaries? Lorne Buchannan was a foul a person as Marjorie had ever met.

She opened and closed her mouth thrice, so utterly insulted she couldn't form words. Surely she gawped like a flopping salmon upon an embankment. She itched to slap his ruddy face and clenched her fan so tightly that the poor accessory threatened to snap in two.

If Graeme or Camden learned of his insulting insinuation, they'd trounce Lorne Buchannan soundly.

Only—they mustn't know.

It would ruin everything—the tentative peace and any hope for reconciliation between the Kennedys and Buchannans. She wouldn't be the cause of another chasm between the cousins. Not when they still walked on eggshells around each other.

At last, she found her tongue. Presenting her chilliest demeanor, she snapped, "I have no interest in dancing with you, Mr. Buchannan. Not now or in the future. Kindly take your leave and do not trouble me with your presence again."

With all the composure she could muster, given her stomach threatened to cast up her dinner and she shook with repressed fury, she presented her back and sought a familiar face as an excuse to leave him where he stood.

The only women she knew, Berget and the lovely Granville sisters, still danced. Perhaps the friendly matron resembling a peacock?

She searched the crowd for Lady Kilpatrick to no avail.

Behind her, Lorne Buchannan breathed in uneven rasps,

and she hadn't a doubt he'd trained his attention on her bottom. The licentious bounder.

Widow's needs, indeed.

If she were a man, he'd now lay upon the polished floor, out cold from the punch she'd have delivered to his face.

"Dinna play sluttish games with me," he growled, seizing her upper arm in a punishing grip.

Gasping and trying to free herself without causing a scene, she poured all of her outrage into the glare she leveled him. "Unhand me, you ill-mannered fiend."

Excitement glittered in his eyes, a dingy, swamp-brown compared to Keane's breathtaking hazel.

He relishes intimidating females.

If her flesh hadn't already been crawling, it would've at that knowledge. Crawled right off her bones and scuttled into the nearest hidey-hole.

His fingers bit cruelly into the tender flesh of her upper arm and she winced. His mouth slid into a twisted, sinister grin. He enjoyed hurting her.

No. It was more than that.

Lorne Buchannan enjoyed inflicting pain on women. It gave him pleasure.

Her mind shied away from the revolting, perverse truth she'd stumbled upon.

Did Keane know?

Good Lord, how could he not?

Why had he invited this monster to the Hogmanay celebration? Because they were cousins? Surely that wasn't cause enough to put his female guests at the mercy of this... This... Villain.

Shoulders squared and her chin elevated, she refused to show her fear. "I. *Said*. Unhand. Me." Panic swirled in her breast. Surely he wouldn't force her from the ballroom. Someone would notice.

Wouldn't they?

Like they'd noticed her earlier today?

Truth be told, Marjorie wasn't altogether certain anyone would be aware if she was dragged from the room and, with every passing second, she regretted the decision to stand near the doors.

"Or what?" he whispered silkily, a threat underlying his deceptive calm.

"Or I'll gladly break every bone in yer hand. Then yer arm. Mayhap, even yer damned face." Keane's throaty baritone wrapped around her as he delivered the flinty vow.

At once, Lorne released her, and she staggered sideways a pair of steps.

Keane's hand lashed out to steady her, but he never shifted his warrior's murderous gaze from his cousin.

Oh, thank God.

Marjorie closed her eyes in a flood of relief so profound she nearly sagged to the polished floor. Instead, she sucked in several short, panting breaths and willed her fear and repulsion to dissipate as she furtively glanced around to see if anyone had observed the exchange.

To her immense gratification, the guests seemed absorbed in dancing and conversing. The woman who'd glowered at her earlier, and her besotted beau, had disappeared. A couple of clansmen flashed Keane a casual glance, but no one's attention lingered. Subtly rubbing her bruised arm, she angled toward the arguing cousins.

"Are ye all right, Marjorie?" Keane asked without looking at her. He eyed his cousin the way a panther might study its prey before going for the jugular.

"Yes," she assured him. "Yes. I'm fine."

Now that you are here.

The cousins looked so much alike they might've been brothers, except Lorne possessed more prominent eyes, a slightly more pronounced nose, and puffier lips. Both were undeniably handsome, but whereas Marjorie felt drawn to Keane's dark good looks, Lorne's appeared sinister and repulsed her.

The chiseled planes and contours of Keane's rugged, sun-browned features invited examination and intimacy, whereas Lorne's pallid skin and watery eyes bespoke dissipation and debauchery.

A shiver crept up her spine.

She truly did not like the man.

"I suggest, *Cousin*, ye retire to yer chambers immediately, else I forget we are kin and toss ye out on yer arse." Features taut and uncompromising, Keane's gaze seared his cousin with accusations and condemnation. "Ye will take yer leave in the morn."

"But... But what shall I tell my father?" Lorne spluttered, glaring at Keane and Marjorie in turn.

"I dinna care. But ken this, when ye assault a guest of mine, ye are nae longer welcome in my home." A thunderous expression descended on Keane's face when he observed her cradling her abused arm. "And when ye injure a guest, my door is barred to ye forevermore."

"We'll see," Lorne snarled, balling his fists. "My father shall have somethin' to say about it. Ye can be certain."

"I dinna care what *he* says." Keane jabbed a thumb at his broad chest. "*I* am the laird and the duke. *My* word is law here. Now be gone," he grated. "Before I teach ye a lesson ye'll no' soon forget."

Loathing contorting his face, Lorne spun on his heel,

except in his pished state, he tottered unsteadily before regaining his balance.

Did Keane realize his cousin hated him?

Marjorie bit the inside of her cheek. Or was the antagonism directed toward her for spurning Lorne's attention?

With a dip of his chin, Keane signaled two immense Scots.

At once, they strode forward and positioned themselves on either side of Lorne. Camden and Graeme were large men, but these two brutes were at least a head taller and two stone heavier. Veritable giants, their chests half again as wide as Keane's.

"What's this?" Lorne spat, his bulgy eyes glinting with rage as he swung his bleary gaze between the two stone-faced Scotsmen.

"Assurance ye go straight to yer chamber and remain there all night," Keane replied smoothly. "If ye make a sound or resist in any way, they are instructed to cast yer sorry arse out the door. Into the snow. Without the benefit of a cloak."

Keane leaned down, his voice lethal, and Lorne flinched, retreating a step. "Nae one will let ye back in, and 'tis a damned sorry night to weather the elements."

Lorne laughed and shook his head. "Have ye looked outside the past hour? Nae one is goin' anywhere. No' tonight nor tomorrow, *Cousin*."

Still chuckling evilly, he tramped away on unsteady feet, listing to the right and then the left every few paces.

Marjorie had examined the grounds from her tower window before coming below. Lorne Buchannan exaggerated greatly. He might be uncomfortable but wouldn't perish if tossed from the keep tonight.

"Thank you, Your Grace." All of a sudden, Marjorie only wanted to seek her bed and pretend the last ten minutes had never taken place. "If you'll excuse me—"

Unexpectedly, Keane extended a hand. "Dance with me, Marjorie." His hazel eyes, the irises rimmed in forest green, softened at the corners and his firm mouth hitched upward. "Please. I have it on good authority ye dance divinely."

Marjorie couldn't say no. Didn't want to, in truth. She'd wanted to dance with Keane since that fateful night last August. And she did so love to dance.

She angled her head as she laid her hand in his. "Whoever told you that falsehood misled you. I am at best mediocre, Your Grace. Unless, of course, you count exuberance, of which I own an abundance when it comes to stepping to the music."

"Keane," he corrected softly. "And I sincerely doubt there's a single thing mediocre about ye, Marjorie."

Startled, she glanced upward.

Lord, he was tall. So tall she had to tilt her head to meet his warm gaze. His request to address him by his given name was too bold, and much too forward too soon.

She demurred. "I'm not sure—"

"We're cousins, are we no'?"

Not precisely. In truth, he was a cousin to her brothers-in-law and no relation to her at all. The disturbing feelings he aroused in her most assuredly weren't cousinly.

Was *cousinly* even a word?

"Surely cousins might address one another by their given names." As he spoke, he guided her onto the dance floor.

Several inquisitive gazes swung in their direction.

Perfectly wonderful.

By singling Marjorie out for a dance, Keane had unintentionally drawn unwanted attention to them. To her discomfit, the midnight-haired beauty swept through the entry at that moment and visibly stiffened upon seeing Keane speaking to Marjorie, her hand upon his arm.

"Marjorie?"

Her name in his honeyed brogue was her undoing. Any remaining reticence melted away, much like butter spread on a slice of warm bread.

"I thought you didn't dance." He had told her as much last August. Except he did dance with his wards, but that was only rarely. It was some silly rule he had, Camden had explained. "'Tis a stricture you abide by, I've been told."

Keane gave her a devil-may-care wink, and her pulse quickened in a fashion more suitable to a debutante than a widow and mother.

"Aye," he agreed smoothly with a disarming smile that made her knees unhinged.

Good God, Almighty.

How could she bear a week of those knee-weakening smiles?

"But rules are meant to be broken," he said, giving her such an intense look that she feared he'd see the attraction thrumming through her, but refused to even acknowledge to herself. She grappled with her overwrought senses, struggling to find a way to diffuse the sexual tension between them.

"I don't break rules, Your Grace."

A slow, sensual smile deepened the grooves at the corners of his eyes.

"There's always a first time, *jo.*"

SIX

Keane's blood still whooshed loudly in his ears and rage sizzled inside his veins, creating a cacophony of primal male protectiveness, blistery wrath, a debilitating urge for retaliation, and an equal compulsion to sweep Marjorie into his arms and comfort her.

Hell, that was a lie. Comfort *wasn't* precisely what he wanted to do to her. *With* her.

A battle raged within him between his desire for her and his vow to not impose his unwanted attentions on her.

Though she put on a brave front, her face was pale as fresh milk and she trembled like a periwinkle-hued, thimble-shaped harebell in a late spring tempest. He'd meant every menacing syllable he'd directed toward Lorne. He still wanted to pummel the scunner, to forbid him to so much as glance in Marjorie's direction.

Unbeknownst to her, Keane had covertly observed her since she entered the great hall for dinner, a vision in green and gold. He'd believed her lovely this afternoon, travel-weary and rumpled. The woman—no, the woodland sprite—gliding into the hall had drawn the avid interest of several males.

With a pointed, possessive stare, he'd glowered each man into a silent retreat.

Mine. She's mine.

What the hell was he thinking?

Naturally, she wasn't *his*. Women weren't possessions.

Well, in truth, the law considered them as such, but he didn't. How could someone own another? Subjugate them to their will?

Nonetheless, Keane had all he could manage with his two lovely, headstrong, and—he feared—on the verge of rebellion wards. There wasn't room or time in his ordered life, or his restructuring of the dukedom, for a wife.

At once his thoughts sobered, and his gaze instinctively roamed the milling crowd for Lady Constance. He found her near a refreshment table, a *moue* on her mouth as she frowned her displeasure at him.

God's balls.

Was she the jealous type?

He'd be bound she was.

Should he warn Marjorie?

About what?

By-the-by, Marjorie, there's a woman here with designs on the duchy. She mightn't like the regard I'm showin' ye. Ye best watch yerself. I have nae intention of marryin' either of ye, however.

By the by, do ye ken how to use a dirk?

Marjorie might well laugh in his face. Odd that marriage to her didn't seem quite as horrific as he'd always viewed the institution.

What am I thinkin'? She has two daughters.

He'd practically raised two lasses already. Branwen and Bethea were nigh onto driving him to the brink of madness with their not-so-subtle attempts to manipulate him into expanding their social calendars and hinting that they wanted to wed.

Why did women wish to marry so badly?

His wards had everything they could possibly want here at Trentwick.

Truly? his conscience mocked.

Friends? Beaus? Entertainment? Outin's? Balls?

Yes, tonight was essentially a ball, wasn't it?

Not to Society's standards, but since when did he give a donkey's neigh about any of that pretentious rot? Mayhap since he'd decided to restore the duchy's honor.

Aye, now that he pondered it, perchance a broader social circle for his wards mightn't be such a bad thing.

Och, aye, it would be bad—godawful, in point of fact— but he could utilize their introduction to Society as a means to reestablish the dukedom's good name and status with influential peers.

"Why, you're not a cold-hearted brute at all."

Marjorie's exclamation from earlier filtered back to him.

She'd thought him a brute?

He supposed he deserved that assessment. He *had* behaved rather brutishly.

What to do about the delectable woman on his arm?

He glanced down, taking in the lustrous copper head that just reached his shoulder. Marjorie neither wore a wig nor powdered her hair. Two absurd fashions he eschewed as well. In that, they were alike. In a very short time, he'd discovered much to admire and appreciate about Marjorie Kennedy.

And not fifteen minutes ago, he'd heard Lady Kilpatrick remarking to a pair of her cronies as the tower of feathers topping her wig jiggled with her animation that, apparently, he'd staked a claim on the Kennedy widow. *Ballocks.* He'd done no such thing. He'd merely warned opportunistic Scots away from her.

That was all.

Why did men always assume a widow was eager for their sexual attention?

His blood boiled again, and a crease appeared between Marjorie's luminous brown eyes as they took their places for the set. "Keane? Is something amiss?"

Bloody hell, aye.

His cousin had acted like an arse, and now Keane would have his uncle's wrath directed at him. Uncle Bothan turned a blind eye to Lorne's faults, which was partially why his cousin had become an unruly whoremonger. "Nae. I'm still fumin' about my cousin's treatment of ye, 'tis all. I still itch to thrash him."

She offered a nascent smile but didn't deny her upset. "I confess, I'm rather rattled myself yet."

Blinding fury had consumed him when Lorne grabbed her. Instead of creating a monumental scene, she'd tried to extricate herself discretely.

If Keane hadn't been watching her...

His gut flopped over at the ugly thought. Aye, he'd banish Lorne from Trentwick. He'd not welcome a despoiler of women beneath his roof, cousin or not. "'Tis nae wonder. Ye handled yerself with admirable aplomb."

"Do you truly think so?" she wrinkled her nose. "I think I should've been more assertive early on. Nipped Mr. Buchannan's attentions in the bud, as it were. Instead, I do what I generally do. Retreat into politesse."

"Aye, I do think so," he insisted.

She glowed under his praise, her eyes shining with pleasure. "Oh?"

Did no one ever compliment her?

"'Tis nae an easy task wardin' off a drunkard without drawin' the eye of every person in attendance," he went on.

She gave a self-conscious lift of her shoulder. "Ah, but in case you haven't detected, I'm rather invisible despite this." She fluttered long, elegant fingers toward the bright red curls topping her head and gracing her left shoulder. Her hair shimmered like lustrous flames in the candlelight.

"I canna fathom it," he denied.

And he couldn't. He could scarce tear his eyes from Marjorie.

How could anyone ignore her?

She consumed way more of his thoughts and attention than she ought.

He should be attending to his guests, seeking alliances, monitoring his wards. Looking over the crowd, he spied them happily chatting and—by damn, flirting! *Flirting!*—with Camden Kennedy and Bryston McPherson.

A scowl furrowed his brow as his protective instincts kicked into full awareness.

Keane didn't like that. Not one bit.

He blamed those damned new gowns his wards had insisted upon having. When Branwen and Bethea had entered the hall tonight, arm in arm, their faces glowing with excitement and anticipation, he'd bitten his tongue to keep from telling them to return to their chambers at once and don different attire.

Preferably something shapeless and sack-like in a mud-brown or ash-gray.

My God, how was he to endure a week of men ogling them *and* Marjorie?

Dinna forget Lady Constance's petulance.

This was exactly why he didn't entertain or attend social functions.

That last thought brought him up short. At once, Keane smoothed his features. He would manage. He was a duke and a laird. Monitoring his wards and assuring Marjorie wasn't harassed couldn't be all that difficult.

The music for the Strathspey began, and he bowed as she curtsied. The dance steps prohibited anything but casual remarks for the next several minutes. Each time he and Marjorie came together and touched hands, a jolt sluiced through him.

He knew it for what it was. Lust.

Keane hadn't slaked his carnal appetite in a good while, and with each graceful turn and skip of the elegant woman obsessing his thoughts, his hunger to take her to his bed burgeoned. To brush his fingers over her pearly skin and see that splendid mane of coppery hair spilling over her naked body and across his pillows.

He stifled a groan, and she gave him an inquisitive look as the dance steps took her away for a skip and a hop. He ordered the unruly organ at his groin to behave itself, which his cock promptly ignored. It rebelliously throbbed with renewed vigor when he took her hand once more.

A woman like Marjorie expected—deserved—love and marriage.

Keane wasn't capable of the former and wasn't agreeable to the latter. Not now. Mayhap not ever. As a child, he'd learned to shut his warmer, more vulnerable emotions off. After years of doing so, he didn't know how to feel again.

Except if he didn't marry, his wastrel cousin would eventually inherit the duchy. And that he could not—would not—permit.

But for all he knew, Marjorie was still in love with her dead husband—a man known for his kindness and humor. Keane didn't want to address that issue right now. One thing at a time: reestablish the duchy's reputation, and then contemplate marrying—several years in the future.

The music ended and, eyes shining, Marjorie laughed up at him, a breathtaking apparition in her unfettered joy. His gut clenched at the enchanting vision, wanting her more than he'd ever wanted a woman.

He couldn't.

Not a Kennedy.

Not after what his mother had endured at a Buchannan's hands.

He didn't have the right.

"Thank ye for the dance," he said, staring past her. "Excuse me. I have other guests who require my attention."

With that brusque comment, he gave a brief bow and strode away. Before the guilt from the shock on her face at his curt dismissal had him pulling Marjorie into his arms and begging her to forgive him for being a callous brute.

At the edge of the dance floor, he glanced back, unable to resist assuring himself she was all right.

He was ten kinds of an arse, and yet his actions were for the best. For both of them.

She stared at him, one slim hand to her throat, confusion and hurt in her soft doe-eyes.

Then the practiced mask descended upon her lovely features, except for a glint of defiance in her eyes. Turning her back, in a wash of green and gold splendor, she left the ballroom.

At her departure, the room grew dim, as if the sun had ceased to shine.

Instead of playing the host and circling the room to chat with the company, he made his way to his study. Once there, he poured himself a healthy dram of whisky. Eyes closed against the memory of Marjorie's wounded eyes, he swallowed a gulp of the spirit, the sharp sting burning a slow, sizzling path to his belly.

"There ye are, Keane. We need to speak."

Hell's bells.

He stiffened at his uncle's churlish tone. He'd hope to postpone this confrontation until the morrow. Opening his eyes, he turned to face his irate relative and cocked an eyebrow. "Ye've somethin' ye need to get off yer chest, Uncle?"

Heavy brows twitching like an annoyed cat's tail, Uncle Bothan gripped Keane's arm. "Ye've banished yer cousin over that worthless Sassenach slut?"

The air left Keane's lungs in a forceful whoosh and instant ire replaced it. With controlled calm, he stared pointedly at his uncle's hand gripping his forearm, then raised his eyebrows in expectation.

His color already ruddy, Uncle Bothan flushed an unbecoming brick hue, but he stepped backward and released Keane's arm. "Well, did ye?"

"Aye, I did." Keane drained his glass and gave the decanter a speculative glance. *Nae.* He was not his father or uncle. *Or cousin.* After placing the empty glass atop his desk, he folded his arms and leaned his hips against the piece of furniture. "Lorne forced his unwanted attentions on Lady Marjorie and frightened her."

"That's nae what he said." Apparently, his uncle wasn't ready to quit the battle just yet. "He said she teased him, that the redheaded *hoor* wanted it too. Ye ken how women are, Nephew. They pretend nae to want the rogerin', but we men ken they do." He winked and chuckled lewdly. "I like my women to resist. It makes a mon's blood flow hot, if ye ken what I mean."

Keane hadn't thought he could become more enraged, but at his uncle's carelessly slung words, he slowly drew to his full height, grateful for the Kennedy blood that ran in his veins, which afforded him a full six inches over his uncle.

"Lorne lies," he managed through his teeth, despising his father's identical twin more at that moment than he thought possible. "And I have never, nor will I ever, force myself upon a woman." He curled his lip contemptuously. "Unlike ye and yer spawn, I believe when a woman says nae, she means nae."

Mouth pursed, Bothan slid his gaze around the study in the same covetous manner he did whenever he visited Trentwick. "So ye intend to side with the Kennedy wench over yer own kin?"

A Kennedy by marriage only. *That* detail mattered very much.

"I intend to stand on the side of truth." Keane rested a hand on his hip. He should've had this confrontation years ago. "Lorne will leave in the morn. Ye can stay or go, but if ye remain, ye will adhere to behavior appropriate for a Buchannan. Ye and yer kind have done our family's reputation enough damage. And I'll have the name of yer spy in my household while I'm at it."

His uncle laughed then, a guffaw that raised Keane's nape hair.

"Yer as great a fool as Gordan was," he choked out between gales of laughter while slapping his leg. "He could never see the truth when 'twas right under his nose either."

Bothan was either further into his cups than Keane had realized or had toppled over the edge into lunacy.

"Their name, Uncle?" Keane would not be dissuaded. He was done with his uncle and cousin, and the spy must go too.

Finally reining in his humor, his uncle sniffed and waved his hand in the air. "There's been many over the years, beginnin' with yer mother's lady's maid."

"Who is it now?" Keane all but gritted, his patience at an end.

"Yer butler, of course."

Keane didn't believe him. Nevin had been with the family for generations and was as loyal as any Scot ever was.

"Who is it really?" he demanded.

His uncle would depart on the morn too, and henceforth was no longer welcome at Trentwick either. To hell with the gossip. There was no affection or respect lost between Bothan and Lorne and most of Keane's other guests.

Sighing, his uncle shook his head, very much looking like his dead brother at that moment. "*Yer* the grand duke. Ye figure it out."

"Rest assured. I shall." Sooner rather than later, now that he intended to ban his uncle and cousin permanently.

The sly glance his uncle slid him unnerved him.

"Ye ken, I was born a mere two minutes after yer father?" He glanced around the comfortable study once more and rolled a shoulder. So he'd mentioned on dozens of occasions, usually when lamenting that he wasn't the duke.

"I ken." Keane was eager to have this done and return to his guests.

Well, the one person he longed to see would likely be tucked in her bed by now and cursing him to the ninth layer of hell.

"On several occasions, I pretended to be him," Uncle Bothan droned on, his gaze distant as if he looked into the past. "Few but our parents and nurses could tell us apart. No' even many of the staff and certainly no' mere acquaintances or strangers. Gordan would become so infuriated when punished for some mischief or other I'd caused while pretendin' to be him."

"I'm aware," Keane snapped, wishing he'd allowed himself a second dram of whisky.

His uncle took particular glee in the retelling of his misdeeds, as if Keane was supposed to commiserate with him.

Chuckling, Bothan scratched his stubbly chin. "He had the dukedom and all that went with it, just because he was born first. I might as well have had a bit of fun at his expense."

Aye, his uncle had slid into madness. Or did jealousy do that to a person if the emotion was fed and encouraged?

"Think on that a wee while, Son." At the door, he glanced back, his brow puckered. "Yer a far better mon than Lorne. I'm glad of it."

And then he was gone.

What the hell was that all about?

SEVEN

The next afternoon, after a successful morning hunt, Graeme and Camden had joined several of the other more boisterous guests in a snowball fight on the back lawns. Cora and Elana had begged Marjorie to allow them to go outside. With promises their uncles wouldn't permit them to become too cold and wet, she'd consented to their bit of fun in the snow.

Like devoted puppies, Sphynx and Chimera had followed the girls from the keep. Her daughters were as besotted with the wildcats as the big cats appeared to be with the lasses. Perhaps she'd see if Graeme would permit them each a kitten at Killeaggian Tower.

Presently, she sat at the harpsichord in the music room playing her favorite tunes from memory as a few of the other ladies sipped tea and chatted—which was to say, gossiped.

That also included the hostile, dark-haired beauty. Courtesy of Anny, the chambermaid tending the fireplace in her chamber this morning, Marjorie had learned the name of the woman shooting daggers at her with thick-lashed eyes last night: Lady Constance Abercrombie.

A frown puckering her freckled features, Anny had

rubbed her forearm. "She's a mean one is Lady Abercrombie. Pinched me 'cause there werena any strawberries on her breakfast tray. Where is Cook to find strawberries this time of year, I ask ye?"

Where indeed?

Even now, Marjorie felt the woman's venomous, adder-eyed gaze upon her. She intended to avoid Lady Constance Abercrombie if at all possible.

Berget joined her and, with a saucy grin, plopped down beside her on the bench. There was scarcely enough room for them both given the paniers beneath their skirts. A secret smile lit her violet eyes and curved her mouth.

Oh, to be in love.

"I saw ye dancin' with the duke last night." She winked and nudged Marjorie's shoulder, causing her to miss a note. "Och, sorry."

"Shh, keep your voice down." Marjorie battled the urge to slide a glance toward Lady Abercrombie, fearful she'd heard Berget's innocent remark. "The duke was merely being a good host, Berget."

Berget shook her head, oblivious to Lady Constance's flapping ears. "I dinna think so. He didna dance with anyone else." She cast a covert glance around the delightful music room decorated in rich shades of berry and gold. "Several of the ladies have commented on it. And there's one in particular who seems most miffed by that fact."

Ah, so Berget was aware.

Marjorie didn't have to ask which one. Her scalp tingled, and again she wondered if Lady Abercrombie had overheard Berget.

I shan't look at her. I shan't.

Lowering her chin, her focus on the ivory and black keys, Marjorie continued playing. "He but rescued me from a...*deli-*

cate situation with Lorne Buchannan. I believe, as our host, he felt obliged to redirect my attention from the unpleasantness."

She cut Berget a swift glance.

Her amethyst eyes wide, Berget sat upright so swiftly the russet curls framing her face bobbed. She leaned nearer, whispering, "I'd heard he and his father departed early this morn. What happened?"

It relieved Marjorie that Bothan Buchannan had departed as well. He'd seemed too eager to indulge his grown son's whims. Sweeping the room with her gaze, leery of eavesdroppers, Marjorie said, "Why don't we stroll the gallery? We'll have more privacy there."

At once, Berget stood and shook out her rose and cream silk skirts.

Marjorie ended her piece and, amidst polite clapping, hooked her hand through Berget's bent arm. On the lawns beyond the high windows, Chimera and Sphynx romped in the snow, rolling over and over atop each other. She and Berget made their way to the upper gallery, which Marjorie had discovered last night.

"How did ye ken this was here?" Berget asked, craning her neck to stare at the dozens and dozens of breathtaking paintings. "They are magnificent. I had nae idea the duke was a patron of the arts."

Neither had Marjorie.

She'd labeled him a barbaric boor, and the more she'd come to know Keane, the more complex he became. Nonetheless, she still smarted from his abrupt departure from the dance floor last night.

All day, she'd wracked her brain over and over, trying to recall if she'd said or done anything to warrant such a cool reaction. She hadn't. She could only conclude Keane had regretted asking her to dance. And given the aloofness toward her from a few of the other ladies today, she understood why. If he danced with her, politeness required him to do the same with others.

Only he hadn't. And, quite naturally, that had led to speculation.

She'd avoided a scene with Lorne Buchannan only to have her name on everyone's tongues after all. Not only was that disconcerting, but now her name was also linked with Keane's in a fashion she was certain he'd not appreciate. Still, no one had coerced him into asking her to dance.

Just when he disarmed her with his charm and consideration, he became a boor again.

"These are spectacular," her sister-in-law declared, awe threading her voice as she peered at the paintings. "Ye dinna answer my question though."

She slid Marjorie a side-eyed glance.

Drat. Marjorie had hoped she'd not noticed.

"How did ye ken about the gallery?" Berget asked. "I thought the duke wasna takin' us on a tour of the castle until tomorrow."

"I believe that is still the plan." Marjorie considered a painting of a woman holding a chubby babe. "I came upon the gallery last night after I left the ballroom. I couldn't sleep and needed to walk." Because a certain raven-haired, hazel-eyed duke had her at sixes and sevens.

She quirked a crooked smile. "I couldn't exactly go for a stroll outdoors."

At a quarter past eleven. In the snow.

Which was exactly what she'd have done if she'd been at home. Killeaggian's gardens had always provided a peaceful retreat. How many tears had she shed amongst the plants and trees? How many prayers had she sent heavenward while sitting on the stone bench along one side of the quaint wall-in courtyard?

And no one had ever been the wiser.

Worry crinkling her forehead, Berget laid her hand on Marjorie's arm. "Are ye all right? Ye've seemed—preoccupied."

"I'm fine."

That wasn't quite true. But there wasn't an easy remedy for what ailed her, if there was one at all.

Upon hearing the rap of swift footsteps, they both turned. A maid approached and offered a brief curtsy.

"My ladies." She looked at Berget. "Yer husband is askin' for ye, my lady. He's in the red salon." She switched her focus to Marjorie. "He bid me tell ye that yer bairns are in the nursery warmin' themselves before the fire and enjoyin' a cup of warm milk laced with honey."

Graeme would make a fine father someday.

"Thank you," Marjorie said, clasping her hands behind her back and nodding. She'd check on her daughters momentarily.

"Excuse me." The maid bobbed another shallow curtsy and hurried away. Likely with this many guests, the poor servants were run ragged.

"I'd best go see what that husband of mine needs." Berget smiled and touched Marjorie's arm again. "Do ye want to stay and admire the paintin's a while longer?"

Marjorie unclasped her hands. "Yes, just a few more minutes before I go check on the girls. I shall see you at supper."

"Ye ken ye can tell me anythin'?" Worry crinkled the corner of Berget's eyes. "I'm a good listener, Marjorie, and I dinna reveal confidences."

"I know." Impulsively, Marjorie kissed her sister-in-law's cheek. "Thank you."

This inner turmoil wasn't something she could discuss, because, quite simply, she couldn't put into words what she felt. This confusion and frustration and edginess.

With another heartening smile, Berget hurried away.

Marjorie remembered what it was like as a newlywed. To not be able to stand to be apart from Sion. How she'd looked in every room for him, and how she'd missed him desperately even when he'd been away for a few hours.

The pain had faded and had become a cherished memory. But memories didn't keep one warm at night or hold one in their arms. That was one of the things she missed the most. A man's arms wrapped around her, holding her close as she rested her cheek against the hard expanse of his chest. Hearing the steady beat of his heart and smelling his musky essence.

"Have ye picked a favorite?"

Absorbed in her ruminations, she hadn't heard Keane's stealthy approach.

Rather than face him, she angled her head and gave him a sideways look.

His expression unreadable, he observed her, his hands clasped behind him. Today, he wore gleaming jet boots, tight-fitting black breeches, and a simple black jacket over a plain white shirt. He'd eschewed a neckcloth, which permitted the merest hint of raven hair to peek from the gap at his collarbone.

Tantalizing and tempting as Hades.

Marjorie had seen him in plaid, formal wear, and now this casual attire. The man looked positively splendid and too bloody masculine in everything. Yet, unlike the fops and dandies she remembered from her one Season in England, he didn't seem to know or care how he affected females.

Of course he knows.

She glanced down, grateful the saffron gown with its lawn-green overskirt she'd chosen this morning complimented her coloring. Though not popular in either England or Scotland, she liked her bright hair. Her eyes weren't particularly noteworthy, but her hair was her glory. And she'd been mindful not to disparage it or let others do so, lest her red-haired daughters overhear and feel belittled.

Keane waved a hand toward a wall adorned with an eclectic assembly of brilliant artwork. "Well? What do ye think?"

There was a youthful eagerness underlying his casual question. Did he honestly care what Marjorie thought?

A finger to her chin, she studied the paintings. There didn't appear to be a theme or a preference for a particular style, except all were captivating in their own unique way.

"How can I possibly pick just one?" She tossed him a short glance. "Each is beautiful and riveting in its own right, and yet they are so original too."

"Mmm." The sound might've been an agreement or a noncommittal grunt.

Angling her head, she perused a painting of the Madonna and baby Jesus, then turned her regard to an elegant fourteenth-century couple. "You collect what you like?"

An almost boyish smile quirking his strong mouth, he canted his head. "Aye. I've been accused of bein' fickle and havin' nae real appreciation for the *great* artists." Lifting a shoulder, he rubbed his jaw, a slight hint of black whiskers there.

What would it be like to feel that stubble against her skin?

Good God. Where had that come from?

She studied him from the corner of her eye.

Who was the real Duke of Roxdale?

This thoughtful, musing man didn't at all fit with her first impression. Nor the second.

"I dinna care what anyone else thinks." He trailed his gaze slowly over the pieces, pride and appreciation lighting his countenance. "*I* think they are superb." His hazel eyes ringed with forest green met hers, a hint of something tender and alluring within their penetrating depths.

"*Beauty is bought by the judgment of the eye,*" she said softly. "That's—"

"Shakespeare. I ken."

Arms folded and an eyebrow arched, Marjorie looked him up and down.

"You are an enigma, Your Grace. You claim not to dance, but you do so. And with commendable form, I might add. You rescued those huge cats when they would've died and, from what I've observed, you've been an exemplary guardian to your wards. You collect exquisite artwork because you *like* the paintings." She arced a hand in the air to indicate the different sized frames. "And you know Shakespeare as well."

He'd also sent Lorne Buchannan packing for making indecent overtures toward her.

A shadow darkened Kean's features, sharpening the hewn planes. "All are mere trappin's and of nae import. None reveal a man's character, and that's what counts. Is it no'? Make nae mistake, Marjorie, the Buchannans are a sorry, despicable lot. Lest ye forget, I'm the product of rape."

Sobering, and not a little chagrined by her playful banter which he'd not responded to, she slowly shook her head as she considered what he'd said.

"No," she denied carefully. "I'm afraid I disagree. They're a part of what makes you—well, *you*. A person's likes, dislikes, talents, abilities, as well as their faults and flaws. Their life experiences—good or bad. Everything. 'Tis the whole person that captivates rather than one or two attributes, isn't it?"

Keane had drawn closer as she spoke and now put one

finger beneath her chin, tilting it upward. "Aye, but some attributes fascinate more than others."

His unfathomable gaze locked on her mouth, and God help her, how she wanted to feel his molded lips upon hers.

And then, in a heartbeat, they were.

Hard and warm, tasting of mint and whisky and raspberries. As Keane had last night, he smelled of spice and soap, but now a faint aroma of leather and horse clung to him as well.

His stubble lightly rasped her face, and she relished the sensation. Everything about this rugged man oozed primal virility. For the first time since Sion, she longed to join with a man.

Nae, not any man. With Keane. Only Keane.

Marjorie clutched his lapels and his solid arms came around her, holding her in a tender yet unbreakable bond as his mouth ravaged hers. And she welcomed each lashing slant of his tongue, each flaming parry and thrust.

She didn't care that anyone could come upon them. Didn't care that this was utter madness. Her head swam with sensation and his essence and her need. Such an overwhelming need. For him. Only him.

How had that come to be?

"Och, *leannan*," he murmured against her mouth as the fingertips of one hand glided across her collarbone and the other grazed her spine. Her buttocks and then—*oh, God yes*— her aching, budded breast.

She arched into his hand, hungry and eager for his touch. A half-gasp, half-moan escaped her as dizzying waves of desire washed over her again and again and again.

"I want ye, Marjorie." He nipped her neck, and she struggled to make sense of his passion-thickened burr teasing her ears. "I've wanted ye since I saw ye at the *cèilidh.*"

He had?

"Ye smell heavenly," he rasped, his voice thick with restrained passion. "Roses and lemon." Nuzzling her throat, he breathed deeply. "And woman."

He gently squeezed one turgid nipple through her gown, and her knees almost gave way.

Muted male laughter echoed and, with a gasp, she jerked from him, frantically looking in the direction of the sound. Hands trembling, she tried to straighten her rumpled bodice.

"How could I be so stupid?" she muttered to herself. To have taken such a risk? She'd practically let him tup her.

God's bones, to kiss in the gallery with no discretion whatsoever. Like an immoral wanton.

"Here. Let me help ye," Keane said, brushing aside her fumbling hands and making quick work of restoring her clothing to order.

She wasn't sure whether to be grateful for his adeptness or miffed because he knew his way around a woman's garments so well.

He'd just stepped back when a footman bounded down the corridor, his red face perspiring and lined with alarm. "Yer Grace. There ye are!"

"What is it?" Keane asked, instantly on alert.

The footman scarcely flicked Marjorie a cursory glance, for which she was grateful. She didn't need a mirror to tell her Keane's kisses had left her lips swollen. Pray God, her hair wasn't mussed as well.

"The Martins' cottage is aflame." The servant swiped a gloved palm across his moist forehead.

Oh no. Marjorie slapped a hand to her mouth.

"Christ." Alarm pinched Keane's mouth and pleated the corners of his eyes. "Alert the clansmen and anyone else who is willin' to help fight the blaze, Ned."

EIGHT

The clock had long since struck one in the morning before Keane trudged up Trentwick's entry. Soot-covered, his clothing torn, and his eyes and lungs burning from acrid smoke, he'd been amongst the last to leave what little remained of the Martins' charred cottage.

Stifling a yawn, he raked a hand through his filthy hair as he took in the bedchamber his housekeeper had assigned to the Martins.

A single curtained bed dominated the room. A toasty fire crackled in the hearth, and candles glowed on bedside tables, in sconces above the fireplace, and atop a table situated before the window. Plates of food also topped the table, and the Martins' young sons' attention repeatedly gravitated to what was, no doubt, a feast to them.

Smiling indulgently, he gestured toward the table. "Help yerselves, lads."

After a hesitant glance toward their parents and receiving confirming nods, Toby and Eric rushed to the table. With awe-widened eyes and whispering excitedly to each other, they reverently examined each plate.

"What do ye say?" their mother admonished, hands on her ample hips and fair brows high on her forehead.

"Thank ye, Yer Grace," the lads said in unison. Upon receiving another nod from their mother, they turned their awestruck gazes to the food once more.

Keane scanned the room again. With the additional servants his Hogmanay guests had brought with them, there wasn't a private servant's room available. Feeling certain the Martins would prefer privacy in any event, he'd specifically requested one of Trentwick's simpler bedchambers.

The Martins were uncomfortable enough accepting their laird's hospitality, and a fancier room would've increased their discomfit. As it was, this chamber was nearly half the size of the Martins' humble cottage, the remnants of which now smoldered a mile away.

"Mrs. Martin, yer lads are welcome to sleep in the nursery after they eat and bathe, or I can request a separate chamber for them if ye wish," Keane offered, his attention on the only bed while he tried not to wrinkle his nose at his own stench.

"Thank ye, laird, but I'd prefer to keep my lads near me if 'tis all the same to ye."

A gentle and soft-spoken woman, Alice Martin had just lost all of her worldly possessions. Naturally, she wanted her boys close. Understandable, poor woman. She hadn't cried or wailed her anguish at the loss.

Showing a degree of stoicism Keane couldn't help but admire, she'd summoned a hollow version of a smile and said, "As long as Will and the lads are well, I am content."

Keane strode to the open doorway and hailed a passing maid. "Please have two pallets brought up, as well as changes in clothin' and soap and hot water for the Martins." Surely they were as eager as he to rid themselves of the grime covering their persons.

"Aye, Yer Grace." Anny hurried away.

After this house party ended, he'd give his staff an increase in wages. They'd earned it, except for the spy in their midst. He'd had no time to ferret out that rat as yet.

Will cleared his throat. "Yer Grace?

Facing him, Keane took in the man's bowed head, furrowed forehead, and the way he crushed his cap in his work-worn and calloused hands. "I ken the cottage is gone, but I'll pay the rents. And I can still farm the lands and oversee the livestock. And we dinna need to stay here. We can camp—"

His wife winced, then quickly schooled her plump features.

Keane didn't blame her. Camping outdoors during a Highland winter was not something even a hardened warrior would relish. He'd permit no such thing.

Glancing about the chamber, Will swallowed. He paused as his gaze came to rest on his sons, who'd greedily tucked into the fare and now chomped, happy smiles bending their mouths.

"I'll see to the rebuildin' of yer cottage, Will. Ye needna fear on that account." Keane understood how hard it was for this proud man to accept charity. "'Tis the laird's responsibility, and ye and yer family are welcome to stay here until 'tis finished."

Toby and Eric exchanged excited looks before digging into their food once more.

Alice offered a shy, appreciative upward arc of her mouth. "I could help in the kitchens, or wherever else ye might need an extra hand, laird."

Will bathed her with a doting smile. "Aye, nae one makes rumbledethumps as good as my Alice."

"I'm sure Mrs. Dunlap would be grateful for the help,"

Keane said, glad to have settled the matter of where they'd stay during the rebuilding of their cottage.

Will shifted his feet back and forth. "I'm indebted to ye, Yer Grace."

Keane clasped the man's blackened hand. "Ye've always been an exemplary tenant, Will. Ye needna fear I'll turn ye and yer family out for aught that wasna yer fault."

Eyes red-rimmed and his face smeared with soot and sweat, Will looked at his wife and lads. He swallowed, and Keane didn't miss the sheen of tears in the burly Scot's eyes. "Thank ye, laird."

Rage simmered beneath the calm mien Keane presented to the Martins and his bedraggled staff as they rushed about with warm water and linens for the guests who'd assisted in fighting the blaze, including the Kennedy brothers and Bryston McPherson.

The fire hadn't been an accident.

Coming in from the barn, Will had seen a well-dressed man throw two burning wads of some sort onto the thatched roof. He'd shouted at the bastard, and the coward had thundered away on horseback. Will had barely been able to see his wife and sons to safety before the ceiling collapsed.

From Will's description of the man and his mount, Keane knew precisely who the arsonist was. By God, Lorne would pay, and this time there'd be no reprieve for the despicable rotter. Just what his punishment would be, Keane hadn't decided.

Banishment first sprang to mind. He would do it too, but he wouldn't put it past Uncle Bothan to hide his wayward son.

Keane had ordered extra patrols around the castle grounds and sent men to warn the crofters to be extra diligent. He'd also assigned guards to monitor the remaining cottages. Given

Lorne was a slimy craven, he'd not risk getting caught by trying such a stunt again. Not soon, in any event. He might, however, hire riffraff to undertake nefarious tasks on his behalf.

Keane held no doubt the fire was revenge for booting his cousin's vindictive arse from Trentwick, and the unfortunate Martins had paid the price.

"I'll bid ye goodnight then." Keane nodded and let himself out of the room.

Two footmen, each bearing pails of water, trod carefully along the corridor. No sooner had they passed than another pair of footmen, each carrying stacks of towels, rounded the corner. Following them, a bleary-eyed maid toting a basket of soaps yawned behind her hand.

Summoning a sympathetic smile for the weary servants roused from their slumber, he opted to bathe in the loch a few hundred yards from the castle. That was one less bath they'd need to prepare before returning to their beds.

"Might I trouble you for a towel and soap?"

"Of course, Yer Grace," Ned said, handing over the towel atop his stack.

Maggie passed him a small square of soap. "Made just last week, sir. 'Tis scented with heather."

"Thank ye," Keane said. "Seek yer beds as soon as ye are able."

There was no way in hell he'd climb into his bed reeking of smoke and layered in grit and ash. At least the snow had stopped, and tomorrow's festivities could commence as planned. His men had constructed a bonfire earlier in the day, and it sat ready to light during the Hogmanay revelries.

He descended to the first level, his thoughts migrating to Marjorie once more.

Dare he ask her to dance with him again?

He craved her touch, but, more so, yearned to hold her in his arms. Wrap his arms around her and make her his in every way a man did a woman.

He heaved a sigh.

Nae. No' wise. He could justify one dance, but if Keane singled Marjorie out for another and didn't invite several other ladies as well, he invited conjecture. Lady Constance's vexed features crept to mind. She was a perfect example of superficial beauty. She'd been in a pout all day and twice had almost cornered him alone. In her case, *he* needed to guard *his* virtue.

He'd not put it past the woman to press her unwanted sexual advances and then cry foul in an attempt to force his hand. Swans would swim in Hades before he made her his duchess. For his people's sake as much as his own.

He knew full well what a sniping, cruel wench she was.

Only this morning, a maid had rushed past him, chin tucked to her chest, tears seeping from her eyes, and her hand pressed to her reddened cheek. It had taken a good deal of cajoling, but she'd finally admitted Lady Constance had slapped her because she'd attended another guest's hearth before hers.

No, indeed. That virago would never be the mistress of Trentwick.

He glanced into the great hall as he passed, gratified to see the fire banked and the room deserted. Mayhap, except for those servants he'd seen above, the rest had finally found their beds. They'd be tired on the morrow, and he felt for them.

A satisfied smirk twisted his mouth upward when he thought of Mrs. Dunlap.

Keane might've instructed his housekeeper to assure Lady Constance's chamber was the *last* to be attended to each morning, and that Mrs. Dunlap herself would accompany the unfortunate maid assigned to Lady Constance's chamber for the duration of the woman's visit.

Lady Constance might be a shrew, but she was no match for Mrs. Dunlap. His housekeeper could cow the fiercest Scots warrior with a single raised eyebrow. Cross Mrs. Dunlap, and Lady Constance Abercrombie would find her stay at Trentwick most inhospitable indeed.

He let himself out of the keep and walked the quarter mile to the loch, the fresh air clearing his mind.

A few minutes later, having stripped naked, Keane plunged into the loch's icy water. A gasp escaped him on a long hiss as the frigid water closed over his head. Teeth chattering, he made quick work of bathing.

At last, on leaden legs and yawning widely, he made his way to his bedchamber, the soap wrapped in the wet towel cradled beneath one arm.

Utter exhaustion riddled him, and yet he hesitated for the space of three heartbeats outside Marjorie's chamber. At this hour, she'd be asleep, of course. He laid his palm flat against the door's panel.

Marjorie Kennedy. A beguiling enchantress. Nae, a distraction he couldn't afford to indulge.

He shouldn't have kissed her. Nevertheless, what surely must have been an indolent smile tipped his mouth.

Och, I shouldna, but it was pure bliss.

Never had a kiss rattled his senses so thoroughly or whipped a conflagration of desire into a lust-filled wildfire in the span of a single breath.

Passion burned in Marjorie beneath her poised façade. Passion hot enough to rival her flaming hair, and he wanted to take her to his bed and taste every inch of her.

Indulging an imprudent impulse, Keane had asked her to wait up, but he'd arrived to find the Martins' cottage fully engulfed in flames. He wasn't a laird who left his clan or tenants to deal with the aftermath of a calamity.

Just as well, because he didn't know what he'd say to Marjorie.

Certainly not the things she no doubt wanted and expected to hear.

Exhaling a juddery sigh, he dropped his hand to his side and turned away. With pleasant thoughts of Marjorie Kennedy parading through his head, he found his bed and, following hours reliving their kiss and envisioning her in his bed as she slept, he eventually succumbed to slumber himself.

NINE

The moment Marjorie entered the great hall the next morning, she sought Keane. A silent, relieved breath rushed past her lips at the tableau before her.

He sat at the head of the table, the dark blue of his coat giving his neatly brushed hair a bluish tint. Shadows formed half-moons below his arresting hazel eyes, yet he played the considerate host, greeting each guest valiant enough to leave their chambers before noon and join him in breaking their fasts.

His gaze met hers, and the corners of his eyes crinkled in warmth. However, before he could wish Marjorie good morning, Lady Kilpatrick, sporting copious quantities of orange, pink, and yellow silk flowers atop her wig, prodded his arm.

Head angled in the matron's direction, Keane's avid gaze remained on Marjorie and heat unexpectedly warmed her cheeks. He shouldn't look at her like that. Like they shared some great secret—*we do*—or as if he wanted to strip her naked and make love to her on the immense table.

What a wholly delicious notion. But without the guests present, of course.

Taking a moment to gather her equanimity, she smoothed her palms down the front of her ice-blue and ivory gown and arranged her features into a benign expression. These people wouldn't catch her making calf-eyes at the duke. A widow comported herself with more finesse than that.

Berget gave her a cheery little wave and a bright smile. Barely pausing in inhaling their food, Graeme and Camden nodded a cordial greeting. The Kennedy brothers certainly knew how to eat. Sion had been no different.

She made her way toward the remaining empty chairs at the foot of the table. Servants scurried here and there, serving the guests and retrieving more food from the kitchens. They were efficient, organized, and courteous. Trentwick claimed a superbly trained staff.

A pair of footmen cleaned the great fireplace's hearth of ashes, their actions supervised by a hunch-shouldered wisp of a woman wrapped in a worn Kennedy tartan. Her white hair hung to her waist, and the ravages of time had left deep grooves in her aged face. Nonetheless, her faded blue eyes sparked with liveliness, belying her advanced years.

Ah, the duke permitted the redding tradition—the removal of ashes from the hearth as part of the Hogmanay celebration. In all the years she'd lived at Killeaggian Tower, the servants had swept the hearths clean the last day of the year when the family was otherwise occupied.

Did Keane also participate in first-footing?

Probably. Why wouldn't he?

Not only was he the laird and a duke, but he was also tall, dark, and handsome, personifying the luckiest visitor a guest might have after the stroke of midnight.

Giving him a surreptitious glance from beneath her lashes, Marjorie pressed a hand to her quivering tummy. She well understood that sentiment.

Alas, with her red hair, she was the worst guest to have step across the threshold and was thoroughly unwelcome in any home at the stroke of midnight the last day of the year. Though she'd lived in Scotland ten years, she'd never visited a single home for first-footing, nor had she ever been invited to participate.

Scots were highly superstitious.

Sliding her brothers-in-law, currently heartily engaged in clearing their plates, a considering glance, she wasn't certain whether that had been an oversight or a deliberate act.

Although she mightn't believe in the folklore herself, she wasn't so full of self-importance as to disregard or ridicule traditions and rites others highly valued. To do so was the height of arrogance, bigotry, and narrow-mindedness.

Previously, Marjorie hadn't taken offense that her coloring was feared, and assuredly she didn't this Hogmanay either. After all, she had no control over the shade of her hair or eyes.

That was the good Lord's doing and, in truth, she quite liked her hair.

What was more, she made a point to praise her daughters' flaming hair as well, lest they come to think of themselves as inferior. God help the man or woman who belittled either of them because of the color of their locks. No marauding Vikings were going to break down any doors this century, so the fear was misplaced.

A boisterous masculine laugh brought an end to her wayward musings.

After seeing to her morning ablutions and dressing with admirable alacrity, Marjorie had swiftly checked on Cora and Elana. Finding them in the throes of a fit of giggles as they dangled feathers from strings for Sphynx and Chimera to pounce upon, she'd kissed their heads and promised to return later and play for a while before she rushed to the great hall.

A nagging fear that something had happened to Keane, and that was why he hadn't kept his word to seek her out upon his return to the keep, had grown to such an extent that she was practically frantic by the time she'd all but hurtled into the great hall.

Fool, she chided herself. *Keane didn't mean anything by asking you to wait up for him.*

But she had waited, hands pressed to her belly to calm the unease coiling there. Until the clock struck one. Even after dousing the candles in her chamber, she lay wide awake staring up at the pleated canopy. Ears pricked, she'd listened for Keane's knock upon her chamber door.

It hadn't come.

Throughout the afternoon and evening yesterday, Marjorie had discreetly asked several servants if there'd been any word about the fire. No one had information to impart, or if they knew something, they weren't talebearers. Another reason to appreciate Keane's dedicated staff.

She didn't dare inquire about Keane directly for fear of rousing suspicions, but she'd opted to take dinner in her chamber but had then left the tray untouched. Worry had quashed her appetite.

Repeatedly, she'd wandered to the window, brushing aside the heavy brocade draperies, and peered into the starless night. Apprehension, trepidation, and self-recrimination twisted around and around in her mind and middle.

How, in the span of four and twenty hours, could she have gone from thinking Keane Buchannan a colossal churl to fretting over his wellbeing to the extent she felt ill?

Well, that scorching, sense-shattering, knee-buckling kiss might've had something to do with it. Praise the saints, what he did to her.

Marjorie had experienced passion with Sion, but no kiss—

no kiss—had rendered her an incoherent, jelly-kneed ninny. What was more, Keane's kiss had awakened a yearning she'd thought dead. The desire to lie with a man, to wrap her arms and legs about his hard, muscular body and take him deep within her. To experience carnal bliss again.

Slipping into an empty chair beside Bethea, she returned her friendly smile.

"Good mornin' to ye, Lady Marjorie."

"To you as well, Bethea. Did you sleep well?" Amazing how one could carry on banal conversations when every pore, every nerve, every last sense hummed with the awareness of another person a few feet away.

A certain Scot with smoldering eyes and a wicked grin.

"Aye, but I kept wakin' up in anticipation of the festivities." She sliced Keane a covert glance and, seeing him still engaged in conversation, leaned toward Marjorie and lowered her voice. "This is the first time Branwen and I have been allowed to participate in *all* of the merriment."

Her regard strayed to her sister who sat farther along the table. Anticipation sparkled in Bethea's gray eyes when she met her sister's.

"Well, that is certainly cause for excitement," Marjorie agreed, though she'd already decided she'd not be partaking, except for perhaps the lighting of the bonfire.

"Keane's finally realized we're adults, though he's nae happy about it." Shaking her head, Bethea chuckled wryly and picked up her fork. "'Tis far past time, I'd say."

Indeed. Would Marjorie feel the same way about Cora and Elana, unable to accept they'd grown into women? The thought made her heart hurt. They were her very life, her purpose. She turned her attention elsewhere, lest her melancholy spoil the new day.

Smiling inwardly, she took in the other early risers. Since a child, she'd preferred to leave her bed early when the day was young and fresh.

Lady Abercrombie wasn't present. *No real surprise there.* Likely, said lady lounged about in bed till afternoon, propped upon scores of pillows and tormenting any servant unfortunate enough to be at her beck and call.

Marjorie relaxed and applied herself to her food with an exuberance that might've chagrined her another time. But today, knowing all was well with Keane and harboring the secret thrill of his kiss in her heart, she felt a degree of optimism she hadn't in a great while. Besides, she had forgone dinner last night, as her gnawing stomach reminded her.

A few minutes later, Keane stood, drawing everyone's attention. His very presence had the ability to snare regard. Men respected, admired, and wanted to emulate him. Women... Well, from what she'd observed, women just wanted *him*.

"If ye'll please excuse me," he said, pushing his chair back. "As ye nae doubt ken, one of my tenants and his family lost everythin' in a fire yesterday. I thank those of ye who helped battle the blaze." He looked pointedly at a few of the men, including Graeme and Camden. "There are a few details I need to attend to first, but anyone interested in takin' a tour of the keep, please meet me here at half past eleven."

The clock had yet to strike nine, so that gave Marjorie plenty of time with Cora and Elana before the tour. She, for one, quite looked forward to exploring more of Keane's fascinating home, which dated back to the fifteenth century.

What had this magnificent castle witnessed over the decades? What secrets, sorrows, joys, and escapades? Were there secret passages? A dungeon? Most Highland keeps contained both.

Unexpectedly, Keane paused beside her chair, catching her

off guard. "Mrs. Kennedy," he said in that deliciously deep brogue that teased her senses. "Can ye spare me a few moments?"

After casting a swift glance about the table and noting several pairs of avid gazes upon them—including Bethea's and Berget's shining with merriment and speculation—Marjorie turned to meet his gaze, mindful to keep her expression neutral.

At least she prayed she'd succeeded, but from the glint in her sister-in-law's too perceptive gaze a second ago, she mightn't have been as adroit as she'd hoped.

Women always were more insightful about such things.

Folding her serviette, Marjorie nodded. "Of course—"

"Wait!" A voice, grating like old paper crumpling, demanded harshly.

Marjorie jumped, and it took a blink before she realized the aged Scotswoman hadn't been addressing her, but rather the footmen bent on removing the ashes.

Keane placed a calming hand upon her shoulder, and the warmth from his palm billowed outward in waves both soothing and tantalizing at the same time. She longed to lean back into his solid form and absorb his heat.

Breathe in his clean, woodsy scent. Revel in his virile strength.

"That's Dolag," Bethea whispered, leaning near and slanting a side-eyed gaze—partially inquisitive and partially apprehensive—at the feeble woman. "Nae one kens exactly how old she is, but she has the second sight."

Naturally, Marjorie had heard tales of Scottish seers but had never encountered one before.

Shuffling forward, Dolag waved a translucent, blue-veined hand toward one of the footmen holding a bucket full of ashes. "What are ye doin', fool? Ye ken I read the ashes every December to see what the new year will bring our clan."

The footman flushed, his countenance apologetic. He dutifully extended the bucket toward her.

She dipped her hand into the pail and let the ashes slowly sift from her wizened fingers. Squinting, she bent forward, muttering and nodding to herself for an extended moment.

Their rapt focus on the decrepit woman, no one said a word.

"Och. Hmm. Mmm," she mumbled, scrunching her face in concentration. "Uh-hum. Uh-hum."

Was that good or bad?

Marjorie glanced at Bethea and then Keane but couldn't determine from their expressions.

Thin lips pressed together, Dolag hobbled to the second bucket.

The guests had ceased eating, each transfixed on the frail woman's bizarre ritual. Even the servants had paused in their duties and, eyes agog, peered at the crone.

Once more, Dolag dipped her gnarled hand into the cinders. As before, murmuring nonsensical gibberish, her features skewed in concentration, she sprinkled the ashes back into the waiting pail.

"Hmph." A harsh sound reverberated in the back of her thin throat. Evidently satisfied, she brushed her blackened palms together, dusting off the worst of the residue.

Shifting her piercing regard to Keane, her surprisingly lucid gaze bored into his. Dolag's attention shifted to Marjorie for a rather discomfiting moment. An intense few seconds that felt as if Dolag looked straight into her soul and saw every secret hidden there, before she gravitated her focus back to the duke.

Silent and perfectly still, her plaid gripped tightly about her thin form, she regarded Keane expectantly.

Charged with electricity, the air fairly crackled with anticipation.

Did she expect Keane to ask for her interpretation?

Perhaps that was part of the ritual at Trentwick?

Never having witnessed anyone reading ashes in all the time she'd been in Scotland, Marjorie had no idea.

"Will ye honor us this day, Dolag, and share what ye've seen?" Keane asked, a perfect balance of deference, respect, and ducal authority.

For several seconds, Marjorie believed Dolag might refuse his request.

Another few heartbeats ticked by before the seer gave the merest nod.

With a jolt, Marjorie realized she'd been holding her breath, her body tense with expectancy as she awaited Dolag's reply.

Dolag's watery blue gaze circled the room before she began. "Clan Buchannan and the Roxdale duchy will encounter *much* change in the year of our Laird 1721."

Her quavering voice carried to the great hall's farthest corners. Not a sound echoed in the eerily silent chamber. Eyes narrowed, only the irises visible, she stared at a point beyond Keane.

A point beyond this realm.

Marjorie's nape hairs rose, and a shiver scuttled up her spine and down her arms. Rubbing her hands over the goose pimples, she eyed the other Kennedys.

Dolag held their enthralled regard too.

"I see great darkness, misfortune, and sorrow in the upcomin' year." Dolag flicked a boney finger at the first bucket.

The footman holding it paled and beads of moisture popped out on his forehead, and he gingerly held the container away from his body as if the devil himself had cursed it. Or mayhap, hid amongst the cinders, ready to pop out with the right incantation.

A chorus of gasps followed her dire pronouncement, and Bethea clasped Marjorie's hand in her icy one. "Och, nae."

Marjorie gave the girl's hand a gentle squeeze, not ready to accept the sage's prophecy as absolute truth but neither willing to dismiss it outright. There were too many things the Kirk couldn't explain, and the Scots boasted a history rich in lore and mysticism.

At Dolag's pronouncement, Keane's hand upon Marjorie's shoulder clenched for an instant, his fingertips pressing firmly into her flesh before he drew them away, leaving a peculiar bereftness in their wake.

Marjorie looked up at him through her lashes.

The slanting contours of his handsome face had hardened, but he presented a nonchalant mien, his mouth curved into a tolerant half-smile.

Did *he* believe what the ancient sage foretold?

"*But...*" Like a lightning bolt, Dolag's voice cracked through the unnatural silence.

Every eye swung back to the seer, palpable expectation and hope permeating the great hall. This shrunken waif of a woman held the entire room in thrall.

"But," she repeated, her tone softer as she pointed to the second bucket. "I also see tremendous peace, happiness, and prosperity for our people for decades to come."

"That's more like it," Lady Kilpatrick trumpeted approvingly.

Relieved titters and chuckles filled the hall as the men and women looked to each other.

They behaved as if Dolag had awarded them a reprieve from a death sentence.

Camden slapped his brother on the back as he stuffed a chunk of sausage into his mouth, and Berget dimpled prettily at something Graeme whispered in her ear.

"Och, praise the saints and angels too," Bethea said, releasing her numbing hold on Marjorie's hand. "I swear my heart stopped for several beats with her first dire prediction. I saw myself and Branwen shriveled up old maids."

Dolag shambled forward until she stood directly before Keane.

He towered over her shrunken form by well over a foot.

Up close, she appeared even older than Marjorie had first guessed. If this woman were a day under nine decades, she'd forgo breakfast for a week.

She turned those unsettling, penetrating eyes on Marjorie for an unnerving heartbeat and then astounded her by breaking into a gapped-tooth grin.

Marjorie couldn't prevent the answering smile tipping her mouth. There was something endearing about the old woman that she liked.

Dolag faced Keane once more and patted his arm.

"Laird, *ye* shall determine which it will be." She peered up at Keane as if willing him to make the right decision. "Light or dark? Good or evil? Happiness or sorrow?"

"*Me?*" For the first time Marjorie could recall, he appeared completely nonplussed. "Me?" he repeated, cupping his nape and staring at Dolag intently. "Ye are certain?"

"Aye, laird." Her gaze veered to Marjorie once more. Then, in front of everyone, she took Marjorie's hand and placed it in Keane's, holding their joined hands between her cold, frail palms.

"And this Englishwoman is the only one who can help ye."

TEN

Keane kept his face impassive as he released Marjorie's hand, then took Dolag's wrinkled fingers between his. "Thank ye, Dolag. I shall heed yer words."

She'd been correct on too many occasions for him to callously disregard her prediction. And Odin's teeth, her public declaration that the fate of his clan and duchy lay entirely in his hands unnerved the bloody hell out of him.

Not to mention having the audacity to put Marjorie's hand in his.

Marjorie had looked so astounded that he'd feared she might object and unintentionally insult Dolag. Instead, she'd summoned a tranquil smile, though color suffused her cheeks.

He might not believe in superstition, but Dolag most assuredly did, as did many of his people—a great many, truth to tell.

By God, he didn't have to peruse his guests to know several eyebrows had shied high on foreheads—including the Kennedy brothers—at the gesture. Speculation would run rampant now, and there was naught he could do to dam it.

Dolag had opened the floodgates.

Why wasn't he annoyed?

Outraged? Incensed?

Quite simply, Keane had decided this morning that Marjorie Kennedy would be part of his future, and Dolag's predictions had nothing to do with it. The idea had taken root yesterday and had grown stronger and more credible with each passing hour.

Yes, a previous Buchannan had wronged a Kennedy woman, but that didn't mean Keane would. His intentions were completely honorable when it came to Marjorie. He'd be twenty times a fool not to pursue whatever this burgeoning emotion was.

"Och, I ken ye will." Affection softened Dolag's wrinkled visage before she once more focused that acutely penetrating stare on Marjorie. "Ye'll need the Englishwoman's help though."

She wasn't going to let that particular matter go, was she?

Marjorie's eyes widened a fraction and color skated up the gentle slopes of her cheeks again, but she gave Dolag a warm smile.

How had Dolag known Marjorie was English?

He supposed it wouldn't have been that difficult to find out.

The old woman glanced around and her face brightened. "I have a mind to fill my stomach now, lad."

And with that pronouncement, she tottered down the length of the table gathering those foods she fancied into her tartan, then, humming to herself, wandered from the hall.

For the most part, his guests had turned their attention back to their forgotten plates and abandoned conversations. Keane intentionally avoided looking in the Kennedys' direction. He had no desire to see whatever mocking or derisive glances they sent his way.

Leaning down, he spoke softly near Marjorie's ear. Her lemon and rose fragrance wafted from her hair. "Marjorie, might I have that word with ye now?"

He forced his lips into a serene smile and, trying to ignore his ward's probing gaze swinging between him and Marjorie, he pulled her chair out. Bethea had indeed grown up and possessed a woman's intuition, as did her sister.

"Certainly." All lithe grace, Marjorie slipped from the seat, once more drawing the attention of more than a few guests. With admirable aplomb, she kept her focus on him, though in a deferential manner that no one could fault.

For the first time, he noticed the top of her coppery head reached his shoulder, and he was a tall man. Why something so trivial should cause a tightening in his belly, he couldn't fathom.

We fit well together.

Aye, and he'd like to explore just how well they might fit together in other ways too. When they were both naked.

He leisurely surveyed Marjorie's attire. Her gown's ice-blue fabric complimented her flaming hair.

Fire and ice.

Aye, he'd seen both sides of Marjorie Kennedy. The self-contained, cool widow and the passionate siren who'd stoked the flames of his desire. He preferred the sizzling woman he'd embraced in the gallery.

Keane thought to offer her his arm, but, after considering their rapt audience, thought better of it. Enough logs had been tossed onto the fire of conjecture as far as he and Marjorie were concerned. Instead, he clasped his hands behind his back. "My study is no' far."

She angled her head, curiosity darkening her rich brown eyes. "Is something amiss?" she asked, in a voice meant only for his ears. The huskiness of her tone caused his body to stir in ways most inappropriate in the presence of others.

He longed to hear her call his name in the throes of passion.

"Nae." Sending a reserved look around the hall, he silently asked her to wait before asking any more questions. What he had to say was for her ears alone.

After the briefest of hesitation, she followed his lead and nodded. With the aplomb of a duchess, she fell into step beside him, her satin skirts rustling slightly as she crossed the stone floor.

Mere inches separated them. With every shallow breath, every irregular heartbeat, he fought to rein in his arousal. To wrestle the foreign feelings burgeoning within him for this extraordinary woman under control. And with each footfall echoing on the floors his ancestors before him had walked, he acknowledged this was a battle he would not win.

A battle he didn't have any desire to win.

Yet, seizing her in his arms and pinning her to the wall while he showed her with his mouth and hands and body what he couldn't say—was afraid to say—wouldn't gain her favor. Not when a guest or servant might come upon them, and her reputation was too important to taint.

Not just hers, but her wee daughters' too.

The sins of the fathers—or mothers—and all that.

Hadn't he experienced firsthand the repercussions of *his* father's sins?

Nae, when Keane took Marjorie Kennedy to his bed, he'd take his time and explore every last inch of her creamy skin. There'd be no hurried coupling, but a long, leisurely mating.

To distract himself from the lust heating his blood and

weighing heavily in his loins, he silently rehearsed what he wanted to say. When he'd awoken this morning, in those few moments before life's burdens intruded upon his thoughts, the truth had struck him with such clarity that he'd collapsed back onto his pillows.

Then, what surely must've been a ridiculous grin had split his face.

He wanted to make Marjorie his in every way.

For four months, he'd battled the insidious truth. From the instant he'd set eyes upon her last summer, he'd recognized his mate.

Oh, he'd fought wildly against the truth, but much like a drowning man accepted his fate and succumbed to the water, he'd surrendered to the inevitable.

He, Keane Buchannan, Duke of Roxdale, and Marjorie Kennedy belonged together.

Toward that end, he intended to court the mesmerizing Englishwoman. To convince her to become the next Duchess of Roxdale.

Yesterday, he'd thought he didn't have time for courtship or wooing. Couldn't accommodate a wife at this juncture in his life. Because, until meeting her, no woman had appealed to such an extent. He couldn't envision a partner for life until meeting her.

When a man felt the way he did about Marjorie, he *made* a way. Forged his own path. Overcame any obstacle.

Unless, that was, she didn't feel the same for him.

He pushed that abysmal thought to the recesses of his mind. It was too soon to concede defeat. Why, when he put his mind to it, he could be quite pleasant, charming even.

The fire that destroyed the Martins' home and possessions had taught him something. Life and opportunities should be seized and lived to the fullest right now.

Not tomorrow or next year. Or someday. *Now.*

Keane would be twenty times an idiot not to pursue Marjorie. What he felt for her, well, it wasn't common. Now he understood the secret looks Graeme Kennedy kept spearing Berget. Even Will Martin's gaze had frequently traveled to his wife.

He wanted what they had.

That oneness of spirit. The unity of souls.

Marjorie wasn't immune to him. Her blistering kisses yesterday proved that. But how amendable would she be to his proposition?

Kisses were one thing.

A lifetime commitment was another entirely, particularly when she'd loved another.

Love—if that was what this unholy knotting in his belly and cause of his erratic pulse was—was a gift. A treasure he certainly never expected to receive, but he'd not deny something so precious.

Marjorie could only be an asset in his goal to reform the duchy.

She made him want to be a better person.

For her. For himself. For his people.

They walked in silence until Keane opened the study door. After pushing the panel inward and stepping aside, he gestured for Marjorie to enter before him. "After ye, my lady."

The merest wisp of a pleased smile tipping her winsome lips, she glided into the chamber, her gaze fixed upon him.

Mayhap she was as captivated by him as he was by her.

He couldn't prevent the swell of primal pride welling behind his ribs, but he checked his grin. Cockiness wouldn't endear him to her. He knew that much about the woman he intended to make his wife.

Closing the door with a soft snick, Keane then turned the

key in the lock. He didn't want an overzealous servant or probing guest to interrupt this conversation. After all, a man didn't declare himself every day. If all went well, Marjorie would agree to a short courtship and a spring wedding.

Mayhap March. He'd always liked March, when the Highlands budded to life again.

A winged ginger eyebrow quirked in amusement as Marjorie looked from the key resting in the lock to his face. "Hmm, this must be serious indeed if you need to lock me in, Your Grace."

He chuckled and raked a hand through his hair.

Glancing upward, he froze.

Bloody damned hell.

Someone had rifled around inside his study. Several desk drawers gaped open, and papers and books lay strewn about the floor. Even the paintings hung askew as if someone had searched behind them.

For what?

Marjorie's eyes widened as she took in the mess, and she turned in a slow circle.

"Keane?" Her delicate features tense, she cast him an apprehensive glance. "It looks as if there's been a robbery. Did...?" She paled and flattened a hand to her splendid bosom.

God rot him for noticing her breasts at a moment like this.

"Did one of your guests do this?" Her voice strained with dismay, she gestured to the disarray.

"I dinna ken. 'Tis possible, I suppose." But not probable. He pulled his mouth into a rigid line and, bracing his hands on his hips, scanned the room again. "I dinna keep any valuables in here."

While he wouldn't rule out the possibility that a guest was responsible for the room's condition, his gut shouted otherwise.

This chaos had Lorne's revenge written all over it.

But what had he been searching for, and how had he gained entrance?

He and Bothan knew Keane didn't keep money or other valuables in the study. They were tucked away safely in a locked chest, somewhere neither his cowardly cousin nor sly uncle would ever discover.

A quick inspection revealed the tall window at the room's far end stood partially open. Since it latched from within, someone had either used the opening to escape or unlatched it to permit someone to enter.

He'd wager on the latter.

No doubt, the spy in his midst had done so, which reaffirmed his suspicions about Lorne. By damn, before week's end, he'd know who the traitor was and just how long they'd been working for his cousin and uncle. And he'd start locking his study when not in use.

"Perhaps you ought to see to this first, Keane. Our discussion can wait."

Marjorie crouched and started gathering documents, her crimson hair swinging over one shoulder. She'd left it down today except for the sides pulled back into a loose knot at the back of her head.

"There's nae need for ye to do this." Taking one knee beside her, he collected the papers from her grasp.

His fingers brushed her hand, and she inhaled sharply, dropping her gaze.

A satisfied grin pulled the corners of his mouth upward.

He gathered her hands in his, and she brought her gaze up to meet his. "Keane?"

"Leave it," he said, helping her stand. Still holding her hand in his, he led her to the sofa facing the fireplace. Unlike the great hall's fireplace, a fire snapped and crackled its blue and white tiled, freshly swept hearth. "Please sit."

Eyebrows knitted, Marjorie settled onto the plump cushion.

When Keane sat beside her, his thigh brushing hers, her chest rose with another swift intake of breath. She licked her lower lip and then, as if realizing what she did, ceased abruptly.

"You had something you wished to say to me in private?" she asked.

"Aye."

But where to begin?

Just come out with it?

Would that be too bold and put her off?

"Marjorie..."

She went still suddenly, her stricken dark-honey gaze colliding with his. "Have my daughters done—"

"Shh." He put a finger to her lips and nearly groaned aloud at the sensation of the warm, moist pillows beneath the pad. "To my knowledge, the lasses havna done anythin'."

Visibly relaxing, she gave him a weak smile. "Oh, good. I feared they'd managed to embroil themselves in a spot of mischief. They do so with frustrating and clever regularity. Not that they're deliberately disobedient..."

She clamped her mouth shut as if fearing she'd said too much.

Those minxes would keep him on his toes, to be sure. But after practically raising Branwen and Bethea, he felt up to the task.

Keane turned her hand over, resting the back upon his thigh. Tracing a finger along the lines grooving her palm, he said, "There's somethin' ye need to ken. Somethin' verra important."

She studied his face, uncertainty replacing her earlier consternation. "What is it?"

Meeting her inquisitive gaze, he peered deep within those captivating, dark brown pools. A man could lose himself in them. He wanted to lose himself in them as he made love to her.

"I mean to court ye, Marjorie."

ELEVEN

Keane hadn't intended to blurt his intentions, but gazing into her fathomless brown eyes, the words had wrapped around his tongue and he'd forgotten himself.

"What? *What?*"

Marjorie's mouth went slack and she blinked several times, the coppery tips of her lashes fluttering. But not in the manner of a practiced flirt coyly batting her eyelashes. No, Marjorie sought to rein in her astonishment and bewilderment.

She was quite adorable in her bafflement.

"Court me? As in...?" Her bewildered gaze probing his, she cleared her throat. "Um, courtship usually leads to... That is..."

She drew a deep, quavering breath, and Keane forced his eyes to remain on her face and not the rise and fall of her bountiful bosom, which rose and fell rapidly in her agitation.

Pressing her palm to her forehead, she said, "Leads to—"

"Aye, lass. I ken what courtship leads to." Cradling her jaw in one hand, he savored her petal-soft skin against his calloused palm. He wrapped an arm around her shoulders, drawing her near. "And yes, I mean to marry ye, if ye'll have me."

Her lips were but an inch away, so damn sweet and so damn tempting. With a strangled groan, Keane took her mouth, gently prying her lips apart.

Marjorie didn't object or resist but instead sighed and, like dew-touched petals, her lips opened fully. Rotating until her torso was flush with his, she wound her arms around his neck and arched into him, kissing him hungrily.

A firestorm erupted inside him, and Keane couldn't get enough of her taste or scent: roses and lemon. Hitching her skirts up her impossibly long, shapely legs until they bunched atop her supple thighs, he nipped and kissed his way to the lush, creamy mounds balanced above her bodice which had tormented him unmercifully since she'd walked into the great hall.

In one deft movement, he delved his fingers deep into her cleavage, relishing her moan of pleasure when he captured a pebbled nipple. With his other hand, he explored her satiny thigh, moving ever closer to her sex.

Encouraged by her whimpers and guttural sounds of pleasure, he plunged his tongue deep into her sweet mouth, still tasting of the berry preserves she'd spread upon her bread at breakfast.

Marjorie rocked against him, one hand clutching his hair and the other gripping his back. She returned his kisses, matching each thrust and parry of his tongue. They breathed as one, giving and taking, seeking and finding.

He cupped the damp curls at the juncture of her thighs with his palm, and she groaned raggedly against his mouth. Slipping a finger within her moist channel, he reveled in her pleasure as his shaft pulsed demandingly against the fabric of his breeches.

His unruly member would have to wait.

This time was for Marjorie. To show her how damn good

it could be between them. Keane slid another finger into her, and she buried her face in his neck.

"Keane," she moaned throatily. "Oh, Keane."

"That's it, *mo ghràidh, mo ghoal.*" *My darling. My love.*

And then she was convulsing around his fingers.

He pleasured her, rapidly moving his fingers in and out of her slickness while whispering words of passion into her delicate ear. A few heartbeats later, she collapsed against him, spent, soft, and utterly feminine.

Only the *tick-tocking* of the ebony bracket clock atop the mantel and the fire's occasional crackle and pop disrupted the contented silence. Several minutes passed as their breathing gradually returned to normal, though his cock continued to protest its confines.

"Had I known this was the conversation you wanted to have, I'd not have lingered over my breakfast," she quipped before pressing her lips to his jaw in a long kiss.

Unfettered joy flooding him, Keane threw back his head and laughed. She was a wonder. He kissed her forehead, her nose, and then her mouth ever so gently. If the stars aligned and the saints blessed him, she'd become his wife.

Marjorie palmed the granite lump in his groin, glancing up at him with a woman's smile bending her kiss-swollen lips.

God help him. He wasn't a bloody saint.

"Nae, no' this time, love." He lifted her hand and kissed the knuckles before helping right her skirts. "When I take ye fully, Marjorie, we'll be in a bed where I can take my time and enjoy every exquisite inch of ye. Nae on a cramped sofa, fearin' a knock upon the door any moment."

The flush of passion still coloring her cheeks, she sliced a glance to the door. "Aye, that would be awkward indeed."

"I meant what I said, *mo ghràidh.*" He looked at her

intently. "I want to make ye my bride, to have ye at my side forever."

"But, Keane, we hardly know each other." Her gaze dropped to his mouth before sliding away, and she leaned back. "How can you be certain of something so monumental in such a short time?"

He'd expected this argument from her.

"That's where the courtship part comes in," he said, brushing a strand of hair from her cheek, not easily deterred. He'd give her as long as she needed. "No' that I'm no' certain, but I can understand yer hesitation as well as yer desire for caution."

"I... I don't know. 'Tis not just a decision that affects me. I have my daughters to consider too." She straightened, and he allowed her the distance she seemed to need. Forehead furrowed and hands folded in her lap, she shook her head, causing the loose coppery hair to brush her shoulders and back.

Someday, he'd run his fingers through those tresses and spread them over her naked form, and his too.

"We clashed horribly when we first met." She fingered her gown distractedly. "I thought you an utter—erm—pig."

He'd vow she'd thought him an unmitigated, arrogant arse.

"Och, but I believe that's because of the immediate, intense attraction between us that neither of us kent what to do about. I'll admit, it scared the hell out of me, and so I acted the colossal asslin'." With one finger, he turned her face to his. "Are ye afraid for yer lasses? That I'll be rough and impatient with them? I willna, I vow to ye."

"I..." Again, her focus slipped to his mouth, and her tongue peeked out to wet her lower lip. "No, I don't think you'll be unkind to them. I know Bethea and Branwen are devoted to you, even though they think you are overly strict. I suspect you'd be the same with Cora and Elana."

"I would love them like my own."

And he would. Already, the little darling minxes had captured the hearts of his cats as well, and no one had done that before.

"I never thought to marry again," Marjorie admitted quietly, her expression solemn. "I have no dowry or properties to recommend me. Or even noble blood. My father was a gentleman farmer. I'd come to the marriage empty-handed."

"I dinna care about any of that." And he didn't. Compared to love, such things were wholly inconsequential.

One thought niggled persistently, however. Just because her young, delectable widow's body had responded to Keane's caresses didn't mean Marjorie's heart didn't still belong to her dead husband.

Could he accept that truth and yet take her to wife?

Aye, he could, and hope and pray someday she'd feel a modicum for him of what he held in his heart and soul for her.

Keane paused, then ventured, "I ken ye loved Sion verra much."

A wistful half-smile tilted her mouth as she stared into the frolicking fire. "I did. Sion was the love of my youth, back when I had stars in my eyes and still believed in fairytales and happily ever afters."

Life's experiences had stripped her of that innocence.

Her smile turned wry, and she breathed out a shallow sigh. "We only had four years together. It seems a lifetime ago. I see him in the girls." She cut Keane a short glance. "They have Sion's eyes and penchant for his precociousness."

"Och, they do, and they possess their mother's stunnin' hair." He grasped a tendril, looping the soft, burnished tresses about his fingers. "I adore yer hair."

Surprise skittered over her face before a radiant smile illuminated her face. "Not everyone appreciates it. Many think the shade is a curse or a mark of the devil."

"Codswallop," he said firmly. "'Tis nothin' of the sort. 'Tis a gift to treasure."

"Thank you," she quietly replied, her emotion-laden voice husky.

"All I ask is that ye give us a chance, Marjorie. I willna rush ye into doin' somethin' ye dinna want." Unlike his predecessors. But that didn't mean he wouldn't use his considerable diplomacy and seduction skills to woo her.

Indecision played across her features. She was afraid to take a chance. A woman risked everything when she wed. She became her husband's property, and the only rights she had were those he granted her.

Keane released her hair and then, searching her eyes, took her hand and raised it to his mouth, pressing a hot kiss to the knuckles. "I dinna want us to miss an opportunity and perhaps have regrets for the rest of our lives."

A heavy knock shook the door, and he tossed a frustrated scowl toward the din before asking her, "What say ye?"

"I'd like time to think about it, please." It was her turn to put a palm to his face. "I find you devilishly attractive, Keane Buchannan, and I can hardly cobble together a coherent sentence in your presence. But that may well only be lust."

With a cynical, self-conscious smile, she withdrew her hand.

"Ye dinna say." He waggled his eyebrows. "Ye lust after me, do ye lass?"

Her cheeks reddened, but she forged onward. "Don't look so confounded proud of yourself, Your Grace." She poked his chest. "A gentleman never remarks on such intimacies or a lady's private confessions."

"Och, lass, I never claimed to be a gentleman where ye are concerned."

A distinct twinkle in her rich brown eyes, she notched her chin upward and sniffed. "Hmm, I'm not certain whether to be flattered or insulted by your admission."

"Keane." The door reverberated again. "Open this door at once! I must speak to ye. 'Tis most urgent."

Uncle Bothan?

This time Marjorie threw a startled look to the vibrating door. She'd recognized his voice and raised a hand to her throat in alarm.

"We'll speak about my proposal later, Marjorie," Keane said as he rose, mindful to keep his tone from revealing the anger and unease Bothan's presence portended. "Lorne is the rotter who set the cottage afire yesterday, and I must speak to my uncle about the matter." He glanced at the window, reminding himself to secure the latch. "Though, in truth, I dinna ken why he's here."

Should he tell Marjorie that he suspected Lorne was behind the ransacked study? No, it would only frighten her further. To be safe, he'd assign more guards to monitor the castle's interior.

"I must leave anyway. I promised the girls I'd play with them." Having gained her feet, she briskly shook out her skirts before adjusting her bodice. Once more, she appeared the serene, proper widow.

He caught her fine-boned hand in his, running his thumb back and forth across the top of the delicate, white flesh. "Will ye raise a glass with me when the clock strikes midnight? We can toast a new beginnin' for us too?"

Her expression inscrutable, Marjorie remained silent for so long he feared she wouldn't answer. Her eyes softened and, almost shyly, she said, "Aye. I shall be happy to."

Triumph sluiced through him, but he contained the jubilant shout and victorious grin. He'd but won a battle, not the war.

In pensive silence, she accompanied him to the door, but before turning the key, he drew her near, inhaling her perfume. Who'd have believed roses and lemon could smell so erotic? He whispered in her ear, absorbing her woman's heat and fragrance.

"I care deeply for ye, Marjorie. Verra deeply."

He couldn't say love yet.

He wasn't ready.

She wasn't ready.

"I know you do, and you honor me." Touching his arm, her expression serious, she said, "I'm not without feelings for you, Keane, but I need a bit of time to sort things out in my mind. Even you must admit, this has been quite sudden."

Och, she'd arrived but two days ago, and the arrows they'd shot at each other hadn't been of Cupid's variety.

"Ye can have all the time ye need, *leannan*." His sweetheart, forevermore.

If waiting meant a lifetime with her as his duchess, Keane would wrestle his impatience into submission. He brushed the back of his hand over her cheek. "Until I find out who broke into my office, I must ask that ye and yer lasses nae leave the castle without an escort. Nae even to take a walk."

Which wasn't likely since the snow hadn't melted as yet.

She parted her lips as if to object, but he touched a fingertip to the soft mounds, and she promptly snapped her mouth shut. She might not have voiced her displeasure with his request, but her gaze revealed muted rebellion.

"Please dinna defy me in this, Marjorie. I'll assign a guard to ye if I must."

After the study break-in, he'd be assigning extra sentries in any event.

An endless moment stretched on and on, and at last she gave a resigned nod. "All right. I trust that you know best."

Turning his focus to the door, vibrating yet again with instant thumps, Keane asked, "Ready?"

"Yes." She gave one short nod and squared her shoulders.

The key made a soft grating sound as he rotated it, but before he could press the latch, the door swung violently inward, almost smacking him and Marjorie in the faces. He grabbed her, yanking her out of harm's way, prepared to defend her with his life if he must.

Bothan charged in and stumbled to an abrupt halt. Unshaven, his clothing disheveled, and great puffy pouches beneath his bloodshot eyes, he looked like he hadn't slept since he left Trentwick. *Or* bathed or changed his clothing.

"I beg yer pardon." Clearly abashed, he noisily cleared his throat and scratched his head. "I dinna ken ye werna alone."

Keane didn't fail to notice his uncle didn't greet Marjorie, or, in fact, in any way acknowledge her presence. Just like him to carry a grudge and wrongly blame her for Lorne's foul behavior.

"I was just leaving, Mr. Buchannan." As always, she displayed impeccable decorum and by addressing Bothan directly, she'd forced him to acknowledge her. She'd make a splendid duchess.

He dipped his chin, muttering rather sullenly, "Lady Kennedy."

She turned a doe-eyed glance to Keane. "I look forward to the tour of Trentwick later."

With regal grace, she swept from the room in a rustle of blue satin, leaving the faintest trace of roses and lemon behind.

No sooner had she departed than Bothan shut the door

with considerable force. "I came to warn ye, Keane," he blurted without preamble. He looked about wildly, his eyebrows knitting together at the room's condition.

"Warn me?" Keane asked, impatient to continue with the Hogmanay preparations.

Swinging his frazzled gaze back to Keane, Bothan's eyes brimmed with something akin to terror. "Lorne has vowed to get even with ye."

"He's been gettin' even with me for decades, Uncle." As if Bothan were unaware of Lorne's penchant for pettiness and his thinly veiled jealousy. "However, Lorne's gone too far this time. He burned out one of my tenants yesterday. Someone could have died, and this time I intend to banish him for his idiocy."

"Shite," Bothan mumbled, pressing the heels of his palms into his eyes and shaking his head. "Goddammit."

"I fail to comprehend why Lorne havin' a fit of temper has ye so distraught." Eyebrows raised, Keane crossed his arms and regarded his father's twin. Lorne's tantrums were commonplace. "Or is it my intent to exile him that has distressed ye? Ye won't sway me, nae matter what arguments ye might present. He has become a threat to my people and has brought this on himself."

Rather than argue, Bothan scratched his stubbly chin. "What in all the saints happened here?"

"I dinna ken." Keane shrugged, once more eyeing the disorder. "But it appears someone plundered my study in search of somethin', though I canna imagine what. I actually suspect Lorne is behind it, if ye want the truth."

"The damned, stupid fool." His uncle let loose with several additional vile oaths, consternation and fury pinching his face into angry lines.

Keane crossed to the sideboard and, after pouring two

fingers' worth of whisky for himself and his uncle, extended a cut crystal glass toward his Bothan. "Ye look as if ye could use this."

Bothan didn't hesitate and seized the glass, downing the umber contents in one swift gulp. His eyes slightly wild-looking, he shoved the glass toward Keane. "Another, please."

Keane obliged him, narrowing his gaze when his uncle gulped down the second glass as well, then peered longingly at the decanter.

When Keane didn't offer to refill it a third time, Bothan released an exaggerated sigh and banged the glass down upon the desk. He rocked back on his heels, lips drawn into a rigid line, and his eyes downcast.

"Lorne isna furious with ye for banishin' him from Trentwick." He glanced up in contrition. "Och, that isna precisely the truth. He's mad as hell about it. He had his heart set on beddin' the Kennedy wench."

"Watch yerself, Uncle," Keane warned in a low, menacing tone. "I havena forgotten yer previous disrespect toward the woman I intend to make my duchess."

Bothan's jaw came unhinged, and, opened mouth, he blinked like an owl blinded by sunlight. "*Du... Duchess?*" he croaked. Heartily flummoxed, he cleared his throat. "Ye would *wed* the widow?"

"Aye, as soon as she agrees." Resting his hip on the edge of his untidy desk, Keane asked, "Why, exactly, is Lorne in a frothin' dudgeon if 'tis no' because I cast him from Trentwick?"

Bothan's bluster evaporated and his shoulders sagged. He looked every bit his seven and sixty years. Older, in truth. "I fear his rage is the result of somethin' I accidentally let slip."

Expression hard, he surveyed the study, his gaze lingering

on the piles of discarded journals and documents. A muscle ticked in his jaw, revealing his agitation.

Now it was Keane's turn to be flummoxed. Bothan tended to pacify Lorne's childish outbursts rather than cause them. And he never apologized for his son's conduct, but rather made excuses or justified his behavior and actions.

"And ye felt ye needed to warn me, because...?" Keane's patience had worn dangerously thin. He had a castle full of guests, and several things demanded his attention before tonight's festivities.

Again, Bothan eyed the whisky decanter wistfully as he tugged one earlobe. "I... I may have revealed that ye are..."

"I am *what*?" Keane snapped, done with the verbal dancing.

Gulping, Bothan clawed at his soiled, wrinkled neckcloth. His troubled gaze darted back and forth, looking everywhere but at Keane. "Erm, my...son."

Keane went perfectly still, all of the air whooshing from his lungs, his blood frozen in his veins.

Shite. Shite. Shite.

He wanted to smash something. Break every pane of glass in the windows. Hurl the furniture across the room.

God. *God dammit!*

It had been repugnant when he believed Gordan his sire, but the knowledge that this... This... Whoreson of a man, a man with no honor or courage or even a smidgeon of decency had sired him. *Christ.*

He despised the very thought, loathed that he was the spawn of such a devil.

His gaze drilled into his uncle, offering no quarter or mercy, and he recognized the undeniable truth in his contrite expression. Keane flexed his fingers against the urge to throttle this cowardly, craven, despicable bastard of a man. The vile whoremonger who'd raped his mother and kept silent while his twin was forced at blade point to marry her.

Odin's teeth.

Everything made perfect sense now.

Gordan's continued denial of despoiling Winifred Kennedy. The ongoing feud between the Buchannan twins. All of it.

Gut-wrenching wrath enveloped him, and, through gritted teeth, Keane managed, "Pray tell, precisely *how* did *that* conversation come about?"

Ashen, his face damp, Bothan stumbled to a chair and collapsed into it. He buried his head in his hands, his breathing harsh and irregular. "Lorne was threatenin' to kill ye for humiliatin' him. Vowed he'd make yer death look like an accident. He gloated that the duchy would be his since ye werena Gordan's son after all."

Lorne had always coveted the dukedom and all that went with it. No doubt in his twisted mind, the dukedom did indeed belong to him. And Keane supposed it did since Gordan hadn't sired a son. Bothan would've inherited and, as his eldest son, Lorne was next in line.

Except, Bothan's spinelessness and deception had cheated Lorne of what he deemed his right.

"Heartily sick of his envy of ye and his mad ravin's, I... I snapped. Lost my temper." His expression defeated and bleak, Bothan lifted his head. "*Ye*, Keane, are the son I'm proud of, no' that weak-willed, spoiled piece of horseshite. I was well into my cups, pished in truth, and I told him as much."

Was the confession supposed to mean something?

Bothan was proud of him?

Keane cursed beneath his breath and, spying his unfinished drink, quaffed back the whisky. "I assume my *brother* is responsible for this?" He waved his hand in a circle to indicate the wrecked room. "Why?"

He had no doubt Bothan knew the reason.

What had he omitted from his overdue confession?

Bothan didn't even attempt to misunderstand. Slouching into the chair, he kicked his legs out before him and shut his eyes.

Even now, he took the coward's way out and didn't face Keane with his admission. Such disgust riddled him that he couldn't prevent his lip from curling. The revolting sack of dung slumped before him was his father. *My father!*

Compared to this scunner, Gordan Buchannan now seemed like a veritable saint.

God, how the devil's glee must be echoing within the many levels of hell at this moment.

"After ye were born, I wrote Gordan a letter confessin' the truth about Winifred," Bothan said, pinching the bridge of his nose. "Which, of course, he kent anyway. He was nae fool."

"My mother mistook ye for him?" Or had the human turd pretended to be Gordan when he'd despoiled her?

Guilty color suffused Bothan's face, and he opened his eyes.

Well, that answered that question.

How outraged Gordan must've been, trapped by his twin. His *married* twin. A man with a wee bairn of his own.

"I was drunk that night," Bothan admitted.

When wasn't he?

"That's nae excuse for yer despicable behavior," Keane gritted out, flexing his fingers and welcoming the viciousness humming through every pore. The violence kept him focused, forced him to dredge up a degree of control he didn't know he had, or else Bothan Buchannan would be lying on the floor already.

Shamefaced, Bothan scrubbed at his face with a hand, muttering, "I asked for Gordan's forgiveness, though I kent I dinna deserve it. I dinna ken if my brother saved the letter, but if he did, 'tis proof ye are my son. Lorne came completely undone when I told him." He swiped a shaking hand across his face. "Screaming and throwin' things."

"I've never come across such a letter. I doubt Gordan would've saved it, such was his hatred toward ye." Keane poured himself another dram and tossed it back, savoring the burning trail to his stomach.

Or mayhap, he had saved the incriminating missive to use against Bothan.

If so, Gordan had concealed it well, because in his many years as laird and duke, Keane had never come across the missive.

Christ on the cross!

Keane's snapped his head up. "Did Lorne say anythin' about Marjorie?"

"Nae." Bothan shook his head. "His grudge is with ye, no' her."

Keane didn't believe that entirely.

"Ye'll leave Trentwick, now, and I never want to see ye here or on Buchannan lands again." He could scarcely bring himself to look upon the man who'd sired him.

"What of Lorne?" Bothan asked wearily as he struggled to stand, a weak and dissipated old man cracking under the weight of his many sins at last.

"Never fear on that account. I'll deal with him."

TWELVE

Humming to herself, Marjorie secured the fastenings of her heavy woolen cloak as she nodded at two massive, armed sentries before she descended the narrow stone stairwell. They returned her greeting with somber nods. That made ten—no, twelve—additional guards she'd seen about the castle since this morning.

A result of Bothan's visit?

The thought made her uneasy, especially after someone had wreaked havoc in Keane's study.

She hadn't intended to participate in tonight's festivities beyond the lighting of the bonfire, but since her heady encounter with him in his office this morning, she'd had a change of plans.

Besides, hadn't she promised to toast the new year with him?

Expectation made her tummy turn over.

She hadn't been this giddy in a long while, and she wouldn't attempt to deceive herself. Keane was the cause. It wasn't just his undeniable good looks and magnificent physique, though she admired both. It was discovering who he was as a man, as a person, that had her bewitched.

She'd misjudged him. Neither of them had been on their best behavior all those months ago, but since he'd so charmingly introduced his cats to her daughters, her heart—and other parts too—had quite decided they liked the duke. Very much, in truth.

His wife.

Keane had declared he wanted to marry her. How could the idea both thrill and terrify her at once? Nonetheless, the notion took root, spreading like the early morning mist rising from a loch.

No opportunities to be alone together had presented themselves the rest of the day, which was just as well. It had given her time to deliberate his suggestion. Certainly, it was far too soon to consider marriage, but a courtship?

Her heart skipped a beat, and a jubilant smile tugged the corners of her mouth upward. Aye, a courtship wasn't at all objectionable. Not at all. It still rather befuddled her to admit she'd caught Keane's regard.

Thus, after settling her worn-out daughters into their comfortable beds and telling them a story interrupted intermittently by loud purrs and an occasional chirp from Sphynx or Chimera, they'd drifted off to sleep.

Playing with the cats all day had not only exhausted Cora and Elana, but the big cats too. And since the girls couldn't claim a single scratch or nip from the oversized tabbies, Marjorie now trusted them.

Keane hadn't exaggerated how tame they were.

She'd asked Phemie to find her if her daughters awoke and needed her.

The lighting of the bonfire would take place at nine. A

glance at the mahogany longcase clock standing proudly in the corridor revealed Marjorie had just over an hour to spare. She frowned upon noticing four more heavily armed guards as she made the landing.

That, along with Keane's admonition she not leave the keep unaccompanied only served to cause all sorts of fanciful imaginings. Giving a mental shake, for surely Keane would advise her if there was a need for concern, she brought her wayward musings back to the present.

Likely, as the security was only on the levels where many of the guests were as well, he'd been concerned that merry-makers would find their way into the keep tonight. A belly full of spirits might cause wayward revelers to wander where they ought not.

How ridiculous her dread of spending Hogmanay at Trentwick and seeing the Duke of Roxdale had proven. Thank God she'd come, for this burgeoning warmth building inside her might very well be love.

Love

Could she truly be so fortunate as to find love not once but twice in a lifetime? And this consuming emotion was, well...*consuming*. Her girlhood love for Sion had been real: sweet, pure, and uncomplicated. But these feelings for Keane might very well be her undoing.

In no way would she describe them as sweet or simple. He'd ignited an inferno in her, and no matter which way she looked at the situation—the possibility of a union with him—the situation was complex.

He'd been right, however, when he'd said there'd been an immediate, overwhelming spark between then. And Marjorie desperately wanted to explore whatever this was, yet she was also afraid.

Afraid of having her heart shattered again because she wasn't a woman who did anything by half-measures. If she allowed herself to love Keane, she'd do so with her every breath, each beat of her heart, and her very soul.

She very much feared she was halfway in love with him already. Being with Keane infused her with a feeling of completion—that he understood her in a way no one else ever had. Not even Sion, and he'd been the best of husbands.

She put a hand to her heart, a sense of wonderment engulfing her.

The greater the love, the greater the risk of pain.

Ah, but also the promise of greater happiness.

Four days remained before they were to return home. A lot could happen in a short period, as she'd already learned.

"Marjorie?"

Lost in her musings, she started when Camden called her name. She looked up to see him, Graeme, and Berget approaching, none looking as cheerful as one would expect for the biggest Scottish celebration of the year.

Smiling, she accepted Camden's extended elbow. "You're a somber lot. Why the long faces? I thought you were eagerly anticipating tonight's revelry." They always had at Killeaggian Tower. She eyed her brothers-in-law, then Berget. "Has something happened?"

"Nae." Graeme's features cleared, and he produced a broad grin as he tucked Berget's hand into the crook of his elbow. "We were discussin' our departure. It would be best to take advantage of the break in the weather, so I think it wise we depart nae later than the day after tomorrow."

So soon?

Dismay shredded Marjorie's earlier joy.

She couldn't possibly make a decision that soon. Shoving her disappointment into a corner of her mind, she produced a bright smile. Nothing—especially thoughts of leaving Keane —would taint this evening.

"I'm glad ye decided to join us after all," Graeme said. "The lasses are abed?"

Marjorie chuckled as she fell into step beside Camden. "Yes. His grace's giant felines have kept Cora and Elana entertained since we arrived. All four were sleeping soundly when I left the nursery a short while ago."

"I'd never have thought the Duke of Roxdale the sort to like cats," Berget commented as they exited the castle. "He seems more like a horse and a dog man. Cats can be quite temperamental."

"He rescued them as kittens. Before their eyes opened, he told me. They think he's their mother." Marjorie lifted a shoulder as they stepped out into the brisk night air. "I suppose he couldn't help becoming attached."

Berget nodded, her face aglow. "Like I fell in love with Frigg's pups."

The puppies had been utterly adorable.

Marjorie looked past Camden's broad form to Graeme. "I was going to ask if you'd consider allowing the girls a kitten or two when we return home? I think it would do them good to learn to be responsible for another creature's wellbeing."

"I havena objection." Graeme cocked his head. "I'm nae sure how the hounds will take to a couple of hissin' kittens though."

"I'm sure they will be just fine, darlin'," Berget interjected. "After all, the dogs are sweet-tempered, and no' all kittens bare their claws and spit."

Five deerhounds claimed Killeaggian Tower as their home. Four had lived there before Berget's arrival. A litter of pups had been born shortly after she'd become governess to Elana and Cora, and Graeme had gifted her the runt.

Smart man. The way to Berget's wary heart had been through that wee pup.

They walked in silence the short distance to the area adjacent to the unlit bonfire.

Nearby, several open-sided tents stood erect. Many contained long tables laden with every sort of food. Others held barrels of ale and whisky, and a few more displayed various goods for sale. Dozens upon dozens of flaming torches entrenched in the ground lit the area and released twirling ribbons of smoke into the night sky.

Where the weak sun had reached today, the snow had melted, leaving the ground soggy, but in the shadows, snowdrifts remained. A slight wind blew, sending the torch flames to dancing and a shiver scuttling down Marjorie's spine despite her heavy cloak.

Musicians played gaily as clansmen and women, villagers, tenants, as well as many of Keane's distinguished guests danced or clapped to the energetic beat. Though the atmosphere was jovial and celebratory, she couldn't help but notice the many heavily armed Scots wandering through the milling crowd or stationed at regular intervals throughout the festival grounds.

A swift perusal of the area and her gaze landed on the man she'd sought—the same enigmatic man who'd commandeered her thoughts all day.

Her heart gave a queer, joyful leap upon spying Keane.

"I care deeply for ye, Marjorie. Verra deeply."

Did Keane love her?

Was that what he attempted to say?

And was that what this enigmatic feeling blossoming in her heart and soul was? She'd been in love before—very much so—but this sentiment was... *More.* She couldn't even find the words to describe the depth of feeling, and a part of her felt disloyal to Sion for even giving the emotion credence.

Keane, a tankard in hand, stood talking jovially with a group of men. As if sensing her presence, he glanced toward her, and a decidedly possessive and provocative smile notched the corners of his mouth upward.

Her mouth swept upward in answer.

Marjorie had tasted those firm lips earlier today, and the experience had been heavenly. Even now, her body ached for more of Keane's touch. For him to take her completely. Heat scampered up her cheeks, though whether from his scorching stare or her erotic musings, she couldn't say.

Thank God, the vacillating shadows concealed her chagrin. But in case they didn't entirely, she tucked her chin to her chest while pretending to fuss with a fastening to her cloak. It wouldn't do for her family to start asking probing questions when she didn't have a ready answer.

Keane excused himself, set aside his tankard and, with those strapping legs she'd so admired, he wended his way between boisterous merrymakers. Not once did his focus leave her, and she cast a furtive glance about to see if anyone had noticed.

Someone had—the singular person she'd not wanted to.

Blast and damn.

Of all the rotten luck.

Emerging from one of the tents, and stunning in a crimson and silver velvet cloak with a silver fox collar brushing her flawless throat, the very alluring Lady Constance Abercrombie *had* noticed.

She aimed her narrowed eyes at Marjorie, spearing her with each blink, and she hadn't a doubt the woman loathed her. She counted herself fortunate she'd avoided any encounters alone with the hostile lady.

To her immense surprise, at that moment, Lady Constance produced a brilliant smile and gave a regal nod of her head toward Marjorie.

She turned to look behind her to see who Lady Abercrombie meant the friendly upsweep of her mouth for. When she found no one behind her, she produced a tentative smile in return. Perhaps Marjorie had misinterpreted the starchy glances from her ladyship.

Didn't some people's resting face look cross or grumpy, when, in fact, they were nothing of the sort? Hadn't she been accused of that very thing herself a time or two, often accompanied by unsolicited advice for her to smile?

Had she misjudged the woman?

Nae, that first night, Lady Constance had regarded her like fresh dung. Marjorie trusted her about as much as a beggar with her purse.

"Graeme, Lady Kennedy, Camden." Keane gave them each a polite nod, displaying his strong chin, before turning the full force of that mesmerizing hazel gaze upon Marjorie and flashing a dazzling smile. "Marjorie."

The sound of her name on his tongue caused her stomach to flip over itself, and only with supreme effort did she keep her face impassive.

At the use of Marjorie's given name, Berget gave Keane a sharp look, her intelligent gaze flicking back and forth between him and Marjorie.

Marjorie could almost hear the wheels grinding in her sister-in-law's head. A nearly imperceptible smile bent her mouth as she leaned into her husband.

"Graeme," Berget said, "I'm rather famished. Shall we see what succulent treats await us? I vow I've never tasted more delicious black bun anywhere. I must have the recipe if I can persuade Roxdale's cook to part with it."

She knows.

Graeme also eyed Keane, though his expression suggested more befuddlement than amusement. "I'm hungry myself," he admitted, still regarding Keane warily.

Likely, he didn't know if he should object to Keane's use of Marjorie's Christian name, which suggested a familiarity reserved for relatives and close acquaintances. But then, they were related after a fashion, and to cause a stir over the matter seemed excessive and pointless.

"Black bun, say ye?" Camden looked eagerly to the groaning tables. "Och, I missed my mid-day meal, and I'm starvin'."

That a certain raven-haired beauty—the ward of their host, no less—also happened to be meandering along a loaded table in a nearby tent couldn't have inspired his appetite.

"I've yet to witness a day ye arena starvin', Camden," Berget quipped, her lips twitching. "Ye and yer brother are hollow to yer toes."

"Aye. 'Tis true." Puffing his chest out, he patted the broad expanse with both ham-like hands. "It takes a good deal of food to keep this warrior fueled." With a mischievous wink and brief nod, he made straight for the nearest tent.

The Kennedy brothers had that in common as well. The mountainous Scots were always ravenous, and their ability to consume vast quantities of food amazed her. Sion had been no different.

It took a heartbeat for Marjorie to realize the melancholy that generally accompanied recollections of Sion were absent. What was more, no sense of betrayal engulfed her, but, rather, anticipation about a possible future with Keane.

A future far different than she'd imagined for herself, but nonetheless quite splendid.

Had she at last finally laid the sorrow and regret caused by

Sion's passing to rest? She'd loved him with a youthful love full of sweet innocence, and theirs had been a peaceful relationship without conflict. Certainly, not this tumultuous onslaught that winged through her whenever she saw Keane or thought about him.

Did she dare hope for a future with Keane?

THIRTEEN

In short order, Marjorie found herself alone with Keane. Well, as alone as one could be in a crowd of hundreds. Yet Keane's regard never strayed from her, making her feel as if they were truly the only two occupying this space.

Again, as their gazes met and meshed and the world went still around them, she tried to put a name to whatever this connection was passing between them. She couldn't identify it, and she scarcely breathed, not wanting the powerful, intriguing link to break.

"Would ye like a cup of mulled wine?" Keane spoke low into her ear, one hand resting on the small of her back. The possessive gesture branded her as his, even through the many layers of clothing she wore.

She wanted to be his. In every way.

"Yes, please," she said, putting into her smile what she wasn't prepared to say in words just yet.

"I should very much appreciate a cup as well, Your Grace."

As one, Marjorie and Keane turned to find Lady Constance smiling at them. Well, her lips curved upward.

Marjorie searched for any signs of animosity on the other woman's features and found only genial regard. Either she was a consummate actress or Marjorie had truly misread her.

Except, she'd been eavesdropping on their conversation, which revealed much.

Keane angled his head, though a glint of suspicion tightened the outer edges of his eyes and mouth. "Certainly. I'll be but a moment."

He sketched a half-bow, and Marjorie forced herself not to watch him stride away. Instead, she watched a rather good juggler entertaining a small crowd.

"We've not been formally introduced," Lady Constance said with only the merest inflection of a Scottish brogue in her refined voice. "I'm Lady Constance Abercrombie. My father, the Earl of Newville, owns the lands adjacent to Roxdale's western border."

Ah, and did papa want those lands merged via a marriage between two noble houses? Lord Newville would find himself sorely disappointed should Marjorie accept Keane's offer. As would her ladyship, Marjorie warranted.

Lady Constance's smile widened a fraction as her deprecating gaze took Marjorie's measure from her uncovered hair to her simple woolen cloak. Though not so much as an eyelash flickered, Marjorie had the distinct impression that despite the woman's amiable demeanor, she found her lacking and inferior in every regard.

It mattered not. Marjorie didn't give a beggar's curse what Lady Constance Abercrombie thought of her. She'd never been comfortable spending Graeme's hard-earned coins on fancy garments and fripperies. It was difficult enough knowing he provided for her and her daughters' every need without being a spendthrift too.

Her expression expectant, Lady Constance plainly awaited Marjorie's deferential curtsy.

She'd wait a very long time. Until the blazing torches about the grounds transformed into flames of ice.

As the widow of a chieftain, Marjorie outranked the woman, but she'd learned long ago those with noble titles generally held very high opinions of themselves.

Instead, she inclined her head. "I am pleased to make your acquaintance, Lady Constance. I am Marjorie Kennedy, of the Killeaggian Tower Kennedys."

"Your accent suggests you're English." One of Lady Constance's finely plucked, midnight eyebrows arched skyward. *In judgment?* "Am I correct?"

"Indeed," Marjorie agreed, determined to be cordial to the difficult woman. "Although I've lived in Scotland many years now and consider her my home. I don't think I could ever leave."

Where would she go anyway?

To her cousin in England?

They still corresponded regularly, but Marjorie hadn't seen Rebecca since marrying Sion. Besides, she wouldn't deny her daughters their heritage or a relationship with their doting uncles.

"Hmm." Lady Constance made a noncommittal noise in her throat. "I should think you'd want to be with your *own* kind."

What the devil did she mean by that?

Ire raised her ugly head and, with considerable effort, Marjorie tamped her indignation down. It took several firm raps to subdue the offense burbling behind her ribs.

She contrived a smile so false she truly feared her cheeks might shatter from the supreme effort to keep it in place. Nevertheless, she refused to voice the retorts parading through her mind, one stinging insult after the other in rapid procession.

Thankfully, Keane returned bearing three steaming cups of mulled wine and saved her. Or saved Lady Constance. After dispensing the wine, he took a deep swallow.

Marjorie forced her focus from the corded lines of his throat. The man was muscle layered over taut muscle everywhere.

He gave Lady Constance a hard stare. "Where's Brixtone? He rarely ventures far from ye."

Was that the handsome man hovering about her ladyship that first night?

Lady Constance's expression turned brittle for an instant, but then she tilted her head and laughed, fluttering her elegant fingers flirtatiously. Naturally, her laugh was dainty and musical. She probably practiced before her looking glass for hours until she'd perfected the melodic tinkle.

Probably practiced that graceful neck tilting and fluttering finger thing too.

"He'll be along shortly, I'm sure," she murmured, giving Keane a sultry look. "As you surely know, Your Grace, Samson is only a good *friend*."

A very intimate friend, if Marjorie didn't miss her mark.

Lady Constance batted her lush eyelashes so rapidly Marjorie hid a smirk behind her raised cup. She inhaled the fragrant steam. The wine was tasty and a perfect remedy to help stave off the evening's chill. And dull one's senses to conniving harpies.

"There you are, Lady Constance," came a male's breathless, slightly nasally voice. "I've been searching everywhere for you."

"Speak of the devil," Keane muttered out the side of his mouth for Marjorie's ears alone.

She checked a giggle as she took in the fop's attire.

He put Lady Constance's elaborate ensemble to shame.

Bewigged, several large stones glittering on his long fingers, he was attired entirely in emerald, green, from his jacket to his ridiculous heeled shoes. Bowing low over Lady Constance's hand, he gave her ladyship a devoted smile. "As always, you outshine the sun, the moon, and the stars, dear lady."

Lady Constance preened as if it were her due, and it struck Marjorie: the man was sincere. In truth, she'd hazard to guess he was madly in love with the woman. From the smoldering, seductive glances her ladyship sent Keane, she didn't return Mr. Brixtone's affection.

Brixtone swung his regard to Keane, and his eyes cooled several degrees in the manner of a male protecting his mate. Only in his case, his gloriously plumed mate had set her sights on another.

"Your Grace." Brixtone's gray-eyed glance gravitated to Marjorie and lingered appreciatively. "Might I beg an introduction?"

Seemingly with a great deal of hesitancy, Keane gestured to Marjorie. "Lady Marjorie Kennedy, may I introduce Mr. Samson Brixtone?"

"Mr. Brixtone." Marjorie inclined her head, aware Lady Constance's agreeable expression had slipped and she now pursed her lips.

Ah, so she didn't want Mr. Brixtone for herself, except to use the man, but she didn't want him regarding any other women with favor either.

At once, a delighted smile wreathed his thin but handsome face. "Do my ears deceive me, or do we share a homeland, Lady Kennedy?"

"You are, indeed, correct. I also hail from England."

"Yes, well, we've established that triviality, haven't we?"

Lady Constance said in a rush, stepping forward and claiming Keane's arm. "Your Grace, why don't we permit them a few moments to chat about their homeland, shall we? Samson was there only last month, and I'm quite certain Lady Kennedy would very much appreciate hearing news of home."

A mere fortnight ago, Rebecca had written Marjorie and she was quite up to snuff on any news of England she cared a whit about.

"Here, Samson, darling." Lady Constance thrust her mulled wine at Brixtone, a bit of the beverage sloshing over the rim and onto his glove. "You may have my mulled wine."

Keane furrowed his brow, giving the gloved hand clutching his arm a disgruntled scowl. "'Tis time for me to light the bonfire, Lady Constance."

"Oh, wonderful. I shall accompany you." The thin-lipped smile she leveled Marjorie might've held a tinge of gloating, but, in the flickering torchlight and with the lack of a moon, she couldn't be certain.

It was as apparent as rouge on a pig, however, that the woman hoped to portray herself as Keane's hostess for the evening.

Jaw flexed, Keane speared Lady Constance another steely look, everything about his countenance shouting she imposed upon him. Nonetheless, either as dense as a turnip or ruthlessly determined, she blinked up at him, all coy femininity.

Another giggle threatened, and Marjorie took a deep drink of the delicious, spiced wine, drowning her humor with the spirit.

"I'll only be a few minutes," he told Marjorie. "Unless you'd care to accompany me?"

Lady Constance formed her mouth into a pout that put a spoiled toddler to shame, and Brixtone glanced away, a muscle flexing in his jaw. Frustration and chagrin rolled off his stiff form in palpable waves.

Poor man.

Marjorie had no desire to spend additional time in Lady Constance's tiresome company. Besides, she hadn't expected Keane to stay at her side and entertain her all evening. After all, he had duties as laird. She'd chat with Mr. Brixtone for a few moments and then go in search of Berget and Graeme. Perhaps she'd have a bite to eat as well.

"No, thank you, Your Grace." Her gaze slid to the woman clinging to him with the tenacity of ancient ivy vines on an equally ancient wall.

"Verra well," Keane said, a knowing glint in his eyes. He'd read her reluctance and gleaned the reason for her hesitation. "I willna be long."

He strode away, making no attempt to shorten his long, rippling strides, thereby forcing Lady Constance to trot alongside him.

Grasping her skirts, she hopped over a particularly muddy patch now and again, nothing the least dignified in her hasty scampering. Had she known she rather resembled a devoted hound, she might've tempered her pace.

"So, my dear Lady Kennedy, what part of England are you from?" Mr. Brixtone asked conversationally, interrupting her wry musings. His chipper tone couldn't disguise the woebegone glint in his eyes.

To love a woman such as Lady Constance could only mean perpetual heartache.

Marjorie had almost forgotten he still stood beside her, so absorbed in Keane's departure had she been. Debating whether to pull her cloak's hood over her head to block the increasingly bitter breeze, she curved her mouth. "My familial home was in Manchester, and you?"

"Lancaster as a youth, and Westmoreland these eight years past. When I'm not in London, that is. I do like the hustle and bustle, the entertainments, and, most especially, watching the gentry prance about full of haughty self-import." He raised his chin, looking down his nose in a pretentious manner before a rakish, crooked smile ruined the effect.

She found herself grinning back at the charming rogue.

"Shall we see what succulent morsels our host has provided for our enjoyment?" he asked, his gaze following Lacy Constance's zigzagging progress.

Marjorie doubted Keane had anything to do with the food. Likely, the ever-efficient Mrs. Dunlap had undoubtedly overseen the preparations.

Mr. Brixtone stuck his arm out in an exaggerated fashion and waggled his eyebrows. "I have a particular fondness for rumdlethumps, though why they call potatoes, cabbage, and onions such a ridiculous name baffles me."

She burst into laughter. "Yes, indeed."

Just as she placed her gloved palm on his forearm, a red-faced maid plowed across the grounds, her brow stitched with worry.

"My lady," she said in a breathless rush as if she'd ran some distance. "There ye are." One hand to her belly, she sucked in great gulps of air. "I feared I'd never find ye in this throng." Her troubled gaze nervously hopped and skipped over the large crowd. "There are twice as many people this year, I swear."

"What is it?" Marjorie didn't know this maid's name. "Is something amiss?"

Had one of the girls taken ill?

Cora had seemed a trifle warmer than usual when she'd kissed her goodnight, but she'd attributed her heated cheek to her bath and romping with the cats.

"I'm Manny, my lady, and aye, there's a wee problem." Her eyes round as saucers, she nervously wadded her apron.

Tempering her impatience, Marjorie prompted, "Which is?"

Manny cut Mr. Brixtone a nervous glance before licking her lips. "Sphynx needed to go outside, ye see. So Phemie took her below and asked a footman to let her out." She paused long enough to suck in another great breath. "She swears she wasna gone more than five minutes, but upon returnin', when she peeked in on the lasses..."

"Yes?" Would she get to the point?

Manny swallowed reflexively before whispering in horrified tones, "Cora's bed was *empty*."

Cora and Elana were not above shenanigans or other harmless devilry.

"Have you looked for her?" Well, naturally they had, else why would this maid be out here?

Manny nodded vehemently, her face waxen and pale brown eyes pools of worry.

"Aye, my lady. Phemie immediately called for two footmen and another maid—me—to look for Miss Cora." She swiped at a tear leaking from one eye. "But we've searched for a half an hour and canna find her." Her tone had taken on a plaintive quality, causing more than one guest to glance in their direction. "So, Phemie sent me to find ye. "

Marjorie's heart stopped for an instant and then stampeded out of control. She was already moving toward the castle.

Don't panic, she admonished herself.

There was a reasonable explanation.

"Thank you, Manny. You may go."

With a sniff and a nod, the maid hurried away.

Perhaps Cora had awoken and, finding the cat gone, went in search of it.

Yes, that was likely what had happened.

"Is there anything I can do?" Genuine concern puckered Mr. Brixtone's forehead as he fell into rapid step beside her.

Marjorie strove to keep the dread from her voice and respond calmly. "Please find my brothers-in-law and Roxdale. Tell them I need them at once."

FOURTEEN

Keane had just lit the bonfire, the flames quickly encompassing the masterfully stacked logs and kindling, when Brixtone urgently demanded his attention.

"Your Grace. Your Grace!" Brixtone said, his tone low and compelling. He'd dropped his air of affected fop, a tapestry of seriousness woven across his features. "A word, please. 'Tis of utmost import."

"Brixtone? Where is Lady Kennedy?" Keane looked past him, searching for her.

"She asked me to find you at once, Your Grace."

His face wrinkled in disgust, Brixtone held one foot aloft, shaking it rigorously in an attempt to dislodge a hefty glob of mud stuck to the sole of his shoe. With a sickening plop, it flew off and landed squarely on Lady Constance's cloak, midway up her thigh.

"You clod! Imbecile. Dolt." Eyes snapping her revulsion and fury, she curled her lips into an unbecoming sneer as she held her cloak away from her person as if he'd deposited fresh cow manure on the fine, scarlet fabric. "Look what you've done, Samson! You've ruined my new cloak."

"I beg your pardon, my lady." Dismay crumpled his features, more for her harsh treatment than any true remorse for soiling the garment, Keane would vow.

"If it cannot be cleaned, you shall replace it. I must find a maid at once." She spun on her heel and stomped away, muttering a string of foul, unladylike curses as she pushed and shoved, elbowing her way through the partygoers.

"Ye were sayin'?" Keane asked, grateful to be rid of the cloying termagant.

Brixtone released a beleaguered sigh.

The man wasted his time wooing that one. Lady Constance Abercrombie might dally with a mere mister, but she'd only wed a man with a title.

"One of Lady Kennedy's daughters has wandered from her bed and cannot be found," Brixtone explained, his forlorn gaze on Lady Constance's retreating form.

Keane didn't bother asking more questions before charging through the teeming crowd. Once beyond the masses, he broke into a run, taking the entry stairs two at a time. There probably wasn't a cause for concern.

After all, he'd positioned watches everywhere.

No' the nursery.

Aye, *not* the nursery, and that was quite possibly a stupid, *stupid* oversight on his part.

Convinced he was Lorne's sole target, Keane hadn't thought it necessary to assign guards to the nursery as well. Marjorie was certain to have fretted if he had, and since there hadn't been a single sighting of the blackguard since the day of the fire, he'd kept the extra security to the lower levels.

Damn my eyes.

He burst into the nursery, expecting to see Marjorie there. Instead, he found two maids hunched into chairs, holding hands, their faces tear stained.

"Where is Lady Marjorie?"

Phemie unfolded slowly from her chair and, voice quavering, said, "We havena seen her." She glanced at the closed door at the far end of the chamber. "Elana still sleeps, though Chimera is also gone now."

Keane wasn't worried about the cats. They could take care of themselves. Should any fool antagonize them, they'd receive a nasty surprise by way of needle-sharp teeth and equally lethal claws.

He advanced farther into the tidy chamber, taking in every inch from the shelves of toys to the rocking chairs placed before the fire burning in the hearth. "Tell me exactly what happened."

In short order, Phemie apprised him of the situation. "I swear, my laird. I wasna gone for more than five minutes. I dinna even go below stairs but handed Sphynx to a passin' footman." She shook her head and, withdrawing a handkerchief from her apron pocket, noisily blew her nose. "I dinna see the lass in the corridor as I returned, so she must've gone in the other direction."

Or had someone made use of a secret passageway and spirited her away?

So far as he knew, only Bothan, Mrs. Dunlap, and Nevin were aware of the passages' existence.

His breath stalled as his pulse ticked up considerably.

Odin's bones, teeth, and toes.

Had Bothan told Lorne about them?

Had Lorne used them on previous occasions?

Perhaps to spy on the activities within the keep?

To spy on Keane?

Mayhap there wasn't an informant at all.

Perchance his wily cousin—*brother*—he'd never become accustomed to that foul truth, had been sneaking around the castle with no one the wiser for years.

Why hadn't Keane considered that before?

What an unforgivable oversight on his part.

Camden and Graeme stepped into the room, countenances attentive and somber. As one, they directed their resolved gazes to Keane, their eyes demanding answers for the hundred questions their disciplined tongues held in check.

"Marjorie sent for us?" Graeme asked, taking in every inch of the nursery just as Keane had, his warrior's instinct evident in his defensive posture and battle-practiced scowl.

Formidable opponents, the Kennedys were good men to have on one's side in a crisis.

"Cora is missin'. We dinna ken if she wandered off in her sleep, or—" Keane cut a speaking glance at the stricken maids, then jerked his chin toward the doorway, indicating he wanted to finish the conversation in the corridor.

At once, their faces impassive, the Kennedy brothers complied, filing out, their huge shoulders filling the doorframe.

Before stepping into the passageway himself, Keane addressed the maids. "Bolt this door after me and do no' open it for anyone but me. Do ye understand? Make sure the windows and other doors are also secured."

The maids exchanged fretful looks but bobbed their heads as they said in unison, "Aye, Yer Grace."

He gave a terse nod and joined his cousins in the corridor. The scratch and scrape of a bolt sliding home met his immediate departure.

Good. Better the maids tremble in fear than make another careless mistake.

Ears flat and to the side, Chimera sauntered down the corridor, her striped tail low and flicking back and forth. She was in a feline snit for some reason.

Where was her sister?

Still outside?

Sphynx detested crowds, and she'd be clawing at the kitchen door in short order if she was.

After prowling near, Chimera nudged his leg hard, emitting a low-pitched growl. Keane didn't have time to ponder what had her riled.

"Go find yer sister." He pointed down the passageway.

With a disdainful flick of her tail and a censuring look from her slitted citrine eyes, she presented her back end and trotted away. Several feet along the carpet, she paused, looking over her shoulder and yowling.

"Find yer sister," he said again. "I havena time for ye right now."

"That creature makes my hair stand on end," Camden muttered, eyeing her dubiously. "I'd hate to have her peeved at me. Are ye positive those cats are domesticated?"

"Aye, but they dinna like a lot of people around. It tends to make them tetchy." Rather like himself. "I need one of ye to stand guard here until my men come up."

Keane indicated the thick panel with a jab of his thumb.

"I shall." Camden volunteered, a hand on the Bollock dagger at his waist. His sword hung at his side, and another dirk protruded from his right boot.

Keane faced his other cousin.

"Graeme, unobtrusively inform my guards inside the castle what has happened and send one to alert the sentries outside that we are tryin' to locate the lass. Have them inconspicuously begin searchin' the back stairways. I dinna want those celebratin' Hogmanay to get wind of this. It doesna take much to send a crowd into a panic. In all likelihood, the child wandered into a nook and fell asleep."

The harsh lines etched onto Camden and Graeme's

rugged faces suggested they didn't believe that the case any more than he did.

"Is Cora kent to sleepwalk?" Keane shifted his gaze between them, his stomach sinking when both shook their heads.

"Nae," Graeme said gruffly.

Och, that would be too damned easy.

"Did either of ye see Marjorie on yer way?" Keane asked, mentally ticking off the most likely routes in and out of the castle, as well as the secret passages.

They shook their heads again, trading tense glances.

Their answer unnerved him more than he wanted to admit, even to himself. So help him God, if Lorne had touched a single hair on Marjorie's or Cora's heads...

There were only three hidden passages: one from the master chamber to the great hall, and another from outside the bailey to the kitchens. That was probably the one Lorne had used *if* he'd accessed the keep. Two sets of back stairways led from the kitchens to other levels of the keep, and that was where Keane would have his men start searching.

The third wasn't truly a passage, but a secret room accessed by panel in the gallery. In prior eras, spies, political refugees, and the like had used the chamber during tumultuous times and rebellions.

He'd shown his guests the smallish hidey-hole during the house tour earlier today.

Cora and Elana had been particularly intrigued and had begged to be permitted inside.

He couldn't deny their big, pleading blue eyes. After procuring a candle, he'd stood inside, holding it high as the girls, their mother, a few of the more inquisitive guests and his cats investigated the space. Elana had whispered to her younger sister, quite loudly, that it was a perfect place for little girls to play hide-and-go-seek.

He doubted Cora, small for her age, could reach the secret latch to open the panel concealing the nook. Nonetheless, he'd search there first. According to Marjorie, her girls had a precocious streak, and the lass may have decided to play hide-and-go-seek.

Pinching the bridge of his nose, he flexed his jaw. "Ye should ken, I discovered Lorne is responsible for the cottage fire, and this mornin' I found evidence that someone had searched my study. My uncle also arrived unexpectedly, in quite an agitated state, and advised me my cousin had vowed to kill me."

No need to tell them Lorne was his brother. Keane hadn't come to grips with that ugly truth. Recalling that cur's blood ran in his veins sickened him.

"Christ on the blessed cross," Graeme swore beneath his breath, bracing his massive square hands on his hips. Annoyance crinkled his eyes and bracketed his hard, turned down mouth. "And when did ye plan on informin' us of these facts?"

Breathing out a long puff of air, Keane splayed a hand across his nape. "I was hopin' I wouldna have to. I dinna believe Lorne's slipped by my guards, and I think 'tis more probable the lass wandered off and couldna find her way back."

If that were the case, where the hell was Marjorie?

FIFTEEN

While Camden stood guard outside the nursery and Graeme hastened to alert the guards, Keane headed directly to the gallery two stories below. As a child, he'd often hidden away in the cupboard-like room. In truth, on many, *many* occasions, he'd avoided stern nurses, punitive tutors, and a neglectful father by secreting himself there.

His senses honed to every creak and groan of the castle, he slowed his pace as he neared the gallery. Head cocked, he listened for voices, the sound of muffled footsteps, or the friction of moving clothing.

Silence met his concentrated scrutiny.

Still, he stayed near the wall as he edged to the short door concealed in the panel. He should've brought a lamp or candle with him. Pulling his dagger from his boot, he inched toward the rectangle cleverly concealed amongst the dark paneling.

A child's frightened cry, accompanied by an enraged female's muffled shout, made him jerk his head up, his gaze boring into the molded plaster ceiling.

Cora? Marjorie?

The sounds had filtered from a chamber above.

Alarm pounded through Keane, scraping his spine with sharp claws of fear and fury, and he cursed furiously when a thump and bang echoed overhead. Sprinting, forbidding his mind to conjure images of what might be happening at this very instance, he bolted to the stairwell, dirk raised and his blood ablaze. His breath rasping harshly in his ears, he made the landing.

A swift, covert scan confirmed the absence of the guards that should've been on duty.

He rounded the corner and pulled up short upon seeing a pair of booted feet. Further inspection revealed McTibbons was only unconscious. An egg-sized lump had formed on the back of his head, but his breathing, though shallow, was even.

Slowly rising, Keane did a swift visual search for the second guard.

He didn't have to look very far.

He found Forbes around the next corner, also insensate, but thank God, not dead. He suffered a gash to his forehead, as well as a knife wound to his shoulder. The bleeding had congealed, but from the size of the slash, he'd need stitches.

Keane removed his handkerchief and, after folding it, wedged the make-shift bandage inside Forbe's shirt, covering the wound. As much as Keane loathed to leave his injured men, at least they were alive, and he was confident Graeme would be along with the others soon.

What was most urgent at this moment was finding Marjorie and Cora. The air burning in his lungs and his heart buffeting his ribcage with the force of a blacksmith's hammer, he approached the bedchamber on silent feet.

Marjorie's bedchamber.

He pressed an ear to the door, almost certain he'd hear Lorne's grating voice. He was as certain his cousin—*brother*— had acted alone.

"You're...mad...I..." The heavy walnut muffled Marjorie's speech, yet he detected fear and rage in her tenor.

"Mama...help...," Cora sniffled. At the sound of her wee frightened, tear-laden voice, Keane erupted into action.

Half-expecting the door to be locked, he slammed his hand down upon the handle even as he kicked with all of his might. The door flew inward, crashing against the wall, causing a stifled yelp from Marjorie and a frightened screech from Cora.

He stopped in his tracks at the macabre tableau before him.

Relaxed and indolent, Lorne sat in a chair beside the fire, an ankle casually hitched on his knee. With one arm, he held Cora's fragile little body next to the chair. He nonchalantly fiddled with a dagger with his other hand, swinging it back and forth, then hitching the blade up and down with his middle finger.

The firelight cast a sinister glint on the red-tinged steel with every upward swing.

"I've been expectin' ye," Lorne said almost conversationally.

Fat tears rolled down Cora's sweet cheeks. Absolute trust he'd save her in her blueberry eyes, she imploringly held her little arms out to him, her lower lip trembling as she whimpered, "Keane."

Not Your Grace or duke or laird. *Keane.*

Lorne shook her roughly, causing another flood of tears.

"He canna help ye, ye stupid brat." He brandished the blade before her terrified face, snarling, "Hold still, or I'll use this knife to carve patterns on yer face or take out an eye."

Her waxen features riddled with terror, the child clamped both tiny hands across her mouth, trying to mute her sobs.

Keane shifted his focus to Marjorie standing at the end of

her bed, hands tied behind her to the bedpost. Her hair cascaded to her shoulders as if she'd been roughly handled or shaken. Or as if she'd struggled with Lorne, which, given the sounds Keane had heard a few minutes ago, he'd wager was the case.

Hadn't he witnessed her mother's fierceness himself?

Her lips bloodied and a welt suspiciously in the shape of a hand on her left cheek, Marjorie's attention never wavered from her daughter.

Silently vowing vengeance, Keane clamped his jaw until it ached to subdue the curses kicking at his teeth.

Brother or not, he'd kill Lorne. Leisurely. Inflicting as much physical and mental pain on the sod as he had on Marjorie and her daughter.

He dragged in a steadying breath, pushing aside his personal feelings. Ordering his pulse back to a normal rhythm, he mustered his control while deciding on the best strategy to disarm Lorne.

Keane was between the hammer and the anvil, and that devil's spawn knew it. He didn't dare charge Lorne. Not with a dirk so close to Cora's throat.

Without a jot of remorse, Lorne would harm her.

"I presume ye've been makin' good use of the secret passages these many years?" Keane asked nonchalantly. "I confess, I dinna suspect ye."

He hoped to stall Lorne and distract him from menacing the wee lass.

A boastful thrust of Lorne's chin and his mockingly skewed eyebrows revealed how much Keane's confession delighted him.

"Indeed. Since Father showed them to me when I was sixteen." He turned his sullen mouth down, peevishness lining his features. "For years, I was at his beck and call, sneakin' in and out of Trentwick. He always thought he had me under his thumb. *Fool*." His lip curled in contempt.

"Where is Bothan?" Keane had half-expected Bothan to charge into this fray. To clean up Lorne's mess, once again. Or was he truly good and done with his despicable offspring?

Instead of answering, a gradual, maniacal smile quirked Lorne's mouth upward. He placed his foot on the floor, all the while twisting Cora's bright red hair between his fingers and trailing the knife tip over the little girl's face, neck, and chest.

Saints preserve us. He is mad.

"'Tis alright, pumpkin," Marjorie crooned. "You're being so brave."

By damn, she was courageous, refusing to show the fear that undoubtedly pummeled her.

"Just stay perfectly still, my sweet, and look at me." She smiled, adoration radiating from her brown eyes. "See how much I love you?"

Cora gave a wobbly nod, her trusting gaze meshed with her mother's.

"Drop yer knife, *Brother*," Lorne ordered, derision and gloating flashing in his demented gaze. "All these years, the wily bastard kept that sordid secret. Can ye imagine how the guilt must've gnawed our father? Now I understand Gordan's rage toward him. Havin' to claim ye as his heir when ye were his twin's whelp."

Marjorie's swift inhalation drew Keane's focus for a fraction. The unasked question burned in her eyes—almost black with terror—as she veered her gaze from him to Lorne, then back to him.

Keane tightened the corners of his eyes in answer, giving an infinitesimal dip of his chin.

Shock registered, and she sucked her bloodied lower lip into her battered mouth, wincing at the movement.

Abruptly, Lorne stood, heartlessly hauling a whimpering Cora before him.

"You monster." Marjorie's throat worked as tears of frustration trailed down her wan face, and she frantically wrenched at the ropes binding her wrists.

Still wearing a lunatic's grin, his eyes glittering with madness, Lorne angled his blade toward Keane. "I'll no' ask ye again. I *shall* cut this wee lass."

Cowering and quivering, Cora released a terrified squeal.

"Shh, darling," Marjorie soothed between the terror strangling her voice. "Mama's right here. Just do as he says."

As if to demonstrate his absolute control and power, Lorne lopped off one of Cora's shiny curls. He dangled the tresses between his thumb and forefinger before tossing it onto the floor.

Fury flooding every pore, Keane advanced two predatory steps, the instinctive, primal urge to protect Cora making him see red. By God, without a speck of remorse, he'd spill Lorne's blood and rid the earth of his putrid presence.

Dual shadows of rage and fear contorted Lorne's face. "Another inch and I swear I'll draw her blood," he gritted out between his teeth. "See if I dinna."

"Mama," Cora wailed, quaking and trembling. "Dinna let the bad mon hurt me, Mama. Keane," she pleaded between hiccupping sobs. "Please help me."

Lorne laughed, a high-pitched cackle. "He canna help ye, brat." In an instant, his features turned to granite, and he pricked Cora's cheek with his knife. "Drop. The. Blade."

Keane let the dirk fall from his fingers, inwardly cursing all the while. Weaponless, his chances of cutting Marjorie free and rescuing Cora diminished profoundly.

No doubt remained in Keane's mind that Lorne had tumbled straight off the precipice into total madness.

Unstable as he was, could Keane reason with him?

Perchance make a bargain?

Mayhap tempt him with something he couldn't refuse?

"Cora and Marjorie have nothin' to do with our differences, Lorne." Keane held his hands out, palm upward. "Let them go, and I vow I'll remain without a struggle."

"Do ye think me that stupid?" Lorne shook his head. "Father told me ye mean to wed the English bitch, and that he hoped ye had many fine sons." His sneer transformed into a feral snarl. "*That* was the last thing the craven ever said."

He made a slicing gesture across his throat.

God Almighty, he killed Bothan?

Was there no end to Lorne's vileness?

Bothan mightn't have been a person worthy of admiration, but to be killed by his son's hand...

Marjorie's horrified gaze collided with Keane's.

He tried to pore all of the reassurance and comfort into his eyes as he could. He would find a way out of this debacle. Somehow. Or he'd die trying.

"Yer a verra bad mon." Cora glared up at Lorne, her little fists rubbing at her wet face. "Ye say bad words too."

Lorne shook her. "Shut up."

She burst into a fresh round of sobbing.

"Shh," Marjorie warned again, her eyes wild as she worked at the ropes. "Don't move, darling. Stay quiet for Mama. *Please.*"

Desperation leeched into her anxious, ragged tone.

Where in the hell were the Kennedys and the sentries?

"They made it so easy for me." Lorne cocked his head and scoffed as he jabbed the tip of his blade between Marjorie and her daughter. "The brat was wanderin' the passages lookin' for her *kitty*. Once I had her in my grasp, her mother was only too willin' to allow me into her chamber. If she'd done that the first night, there'd have been nae need for any of this."

Horseshite.

Pausing, a calculating look replacing his irritation, Lorne gave a sardonic shake of his head. "Och, that's no' entirely true. I canna have ye weddin' anyone, ye see. Why, ye might have bairns. *Sons.* And I canna let anyone inherit, now can I, *Brother*? I'm older than ye, ye ken, and I should've been the Duke of Roxdale all along, no' ye."

Pushing the terrified child before him, using her as a human shield as only a despicable coward would, Lorne angled to the center of the room.

Cora's wee pink toes stuck out from beneath her night rail, and she looked so helpless Keane fought the urge to charge Lorne and squeeze him by the throat until he'd snuffed the life from the rotter.

Something brushed his leg, and he glanced down.

With their predatory yellow-green eyes affixed on Lorne, Chimera and Sphynx padded past him.

"Kitties," Cora breathed. "Stay there, kitties. The bad mon will hurt ye."

As if understanding, Chimera sat, but Sphynx circled Lorne, stalking him.

Good girls, Keane silently praised.

Lorne lashed out with a booted foot, but, with an angry hiss and arched back, Sphynx leaped out of his reach.

Chimera stood, arching her back in warning as well.

"Get those damned cats out of here," Lorne demanded, eyeing the large wildcats warily. Real fear glinted in his eyes. He clutched the dagger with the tip thrust outward as he pointed the blade to the door. "Get them out!"

In less than a blink, hell broke loose.

Sphynx soared onto Lorne's back, sinking her claws and

teeth into him at the exact moment Chimera launched herself at his face.

By God, what an extraordinarily orchestrated ambush.

Arms flailing, Lorne shrieked and cursed as he tried to dislodge the furiously attacking felines.

Keane didn't hesitate. He rushed forward, shoving Cora to safety with one hand while knocking the blade from Lorne's hand with the other.

He pounded to Marjorie and, in three deft strokes, cut her free. With an anguished cry, she scooped Cora into her arms, burying her daughter's face in her shoulder to shield her from the ghastly scene playing out.

Lorne crumpled to his knees amid the cats' furious growls and hisses as they tore at him, unrelenting in their ferocity. Rivulets of blood covered his face, neck, and hands. Yet the cats hadn't gone in for the kill bite, ripping his throat open.

No child should witness such violence and gore.

"Get Cora out of here, Marjorie," Keane ordered, kicking Lorne's dirk across the room. He wasn't taking any chances.

With a swift nod, she fled the room.

"Down," Keane ordered and, at once, the cats sprang free. In truth, as enraged as they were, he hadn't been certain they'd comply.

Teeth barred and still hissing and growling low in their throats, they prowled over to sit beside Keane. And then, as if it were the most normal thing in the world to have savagely attacked a human, they began grooming themselves.

On the floor, Lorne writhed and moaned, his clothing and flesh shredded, and from the looks of him, probably blinded in one eye.

Keane couldn't summon an iota of sympathy. He'd deserved that and more.

Footsteps thundered outside the chamber. A heartbeat

later, Graeme, Camden, and four clansmen plowed into the room.

Marjorie edged in behind them, keeping Cora's cherub's face shielded from the grizzly scene.

"Holy God above," Graeme said as comprehension took root. He gave Sphynx and Chimera a wide birth, as did the other Scots.

If the situation weren't so serious, Keane might've chuckled at the six huge Scots skirting the cats as if they were fire-breathing dragons.

"Remind me never to make them angry," Camden muttered, a good deal of awe coloring his tone.

"They were protectin' me," Cora ventured. "They're my friends, and friends help each other."

Upon hearing Cora, both felines ambled to Marjorie and rubbed against her skirts, loudly purring all the while.

"I think they deserve a special treat for bein' so brave," Cora declared.

Her grateful gaze seeking Keane's, Marjorie agreed. "Indeed, they do, darling."

He read the appreciation in her eyes. And something more. Something that he couldn't explore with her brothers-in-law or his clansmen hauling Lorne's limp form from her chamber.

Her *former* chamber.

Keane would have her moved next to him, assuring her safety. Assuring she was near him forevermore.

Her head resting on Marjorie's shoulder, Cora tipped her lips upward at Keane. "I kent ye'd save me."

SIXTEEN

Lost in thought, a soft pale green wool shawl covering her nightgown, Marjorie sat in a comfortable chair, gazing out the window into the winter night's sky.

Driven by the wind, clouds butted against each other like playful kittens or puppies, but glimpses of starlight and moon-light shone through the vast black space between them. There was something immensely peaceful about staring at the stars while waiting for the man she loved.

Candles glowed and flickered in the sconces, and a roaring fire warmed the opulent chamber. Marjorie suspected this was the duchess's suite.

Brazen of Keane to transfer her to these rooms. Doing so sent an unmistakable message. And instead of pique or vexation, immense warmth curled around her ribs at his daring and presumptuousness.

While she'd tucked Cora into bed once more, servants had moved her possessions. As was their wont, Sphynx had settled beside Cora and Chimera stretched out next to Elana, still fast asleep.

Pinpricks of tears stinging her eyes, Marjorie had run her

hand over both cats' heads. "Thank you," she whispered. "Thank you for saving us."

Sphynx and Chimera *had* saved them.

They might not be as docile and tame as the typical tabby cat, but she'd never doubt her daughters' safety with them again. If she hadn't witnessed their calculated, feral attack herself, she'd never have believed it.

They had known Cora was in danger, and they'd acted together to save her.

It was a miracle, plain and simple.

No doubt Cora would regale her older sister with the adventure she'd had this night. Hopefully, the awfulness would fade in time and not leave lingering scars in her daughter's little mind or on her innocent soul.

Before leaving, Keane had tenderly kissed Marjorie's forehead. "I'll explain everythin', *jo*, but right now my people need me. Their traditions are all some of them have. I try to discover who most needs a first-footin' to encourage them for the next year. This year, eight families have suffered a loss of some sort, so I'll no' be returnin' for hours."

And so, after all of the horrific events that had transpired this evening, he'd painted a pleasant expression on his beloved face and gone to the first-footings. To bring a bit of joy, happiness, and encouragement to others also suffering.

He'd known Marjorie couldn't leave her daughters tonight to accompany him, and he hadn't asked it of her. But next year... She bent her mouth into a secret smile and nestled further into the chair, drawing her legs beneath her. Next year, she'd be at his side, and she'd prove that red-haired women weren't bad luck.

Keane's unselfishness was one of the things she most admired about him. He took his duties as laird and duke seriously and didn't only take advantage of the opportunities those positions afforded him.

He was good. Truly good and decent and wonderful at his core. His gruff exterior protected a sensitive, caring man.

As a child, she'd seen a remarkable stone once. There'd been nothing outstanding about the exterior, but the interior —oh, the gorgeous interior—had been a marvel of purple crystals. Amethysts, her grandfather had explained to her.

Keane was like that marvelous stone, except he also possessed an exterior any woman would sigh over. In truth, the good Lord had taken a great deal of time forming such an extraordinary man.

Marjorie still marveled that she'd ever believed otherwise. Still marveled that he wanted to make her his wife. And she wanted that too. Wanted to spend the rest of her life with him, to bear his children, share his joys and sorrows.

He'd heard the cry of her spirit tonight. Over and over and over, between prayers to God, she called out to Keane in her mind.

Help us. Please. Help us.

She'd never been so afraid. Utterly terrified.

Not for herself, but for Cora and Keane.

God, what a shock it had been to learn Lorne was his brother. There was a story there, and she'd be ready to listen when Keane was ready to tell what, no doubt, was a painful tale.

Sighing, she shifted her position and rested her head against the chair back.

When Berget had joined her in the nursery mere minutes after the calamity had ended, she'd been white-faced and shaking. "Graeme told me what happened," she gulped, her violet eyes awash with tears. "I'm so verra relieved ye and the bairn are safe." She managed an unsteady smile as she clasped

Marjorie to her. "Yer the sister I never had, and I couldna bear the thought..."

"Keane and the cats rescued us," Marjorie explained.

According to Berget, a locked and guarded cell deep beneath the castle held Lorne, his upper body a cartography of slashes, slices, scratches, and bites. Tomorrow, the authorities would collect him, and if he had truly murdered his father, the gallows awaited him.

Never before had Marjorie considered herself an unforgiving person, yet she couldn't summon an ounce of pity for him. Not after he'd threatened her sweet, innocent daughter. The world would be a better place without the likes of men like Lorne Buchannan.

Midnight came and went, but Marjorie didn't seek her bed. Keane had promised to see her before he found his, so unlike a couple of nights ago, she waited.

She had an answer for him. One, she must tell him tonight. She'd wait until dawn if that were what it took.

The clouds shifted again, permitting the quarter-moon to peek through.

Graeme had correctly predicted more charitable weather.

Given the events of tonight, would he still expect to leave on the morrow?

Even if he did, she'd not be going with him. No, this wondrous thing between her and Keane was too precious to abandon. Who had the right to say love needed weeks or months to mature? To be real and lasting?

She loved Keane.

Marjorie permitted her heavy eyelids to drift shut as she imagined what a future with him entailed. More children, hopefully. Strapping sons with their father's glossy midnight hair and charming grin, and another wee daughter, this one a brunette too. Elana and Cora would be thrilled.

Sometime later, she felt a wisp of firm, velvety lips across hers. She curved her mouth upward slightly as she came fully awake, finding Keane crouched beside her, banked embers of desire flickering in his gaze.

"I'm sorry. I meant to stay awake." She blinked sleepily, taking in his slightly damp midnight hair and the day's growth of bristle shadowing his hewn jaw.

His fine lawn shirt gaped at the neckline, revealing a tantalizing display of hair, and the black breeches hugged the splendid, sculpted contours of his hips and thighs. He'd never looked more devilish or seductive, and Marjorie wanted this man with a ferocity that stunned her.

"What time is it?" she asked.

"Almost half past two." He cupped her cheek with his calloused hand. "I almost didna enter, and now I see had I no', ye'd have spent the night curled in a knot. Ye'd have a sore neck for certain in the morn."

Marjorie entwined her arms about the corded brawn of his neck, pulling him down to her. "I never thanked you for rescuing Cora and me."

Ever so softly, she pressed her lips to his, needing his touch, this contact with this man who'd come to mean as much to her these past few days as air or food.

She wouldn't question how it had come to be, but instead revel in the tremendous gift she'd been given—a second chance at love, and a blessing she truly never expected.

"I dinna want to hurt yer poor mouth," Keane whispered, scorching her with his hot gaze as one large hand tenderly framed her jaw.

"You could never hurt me, Keane."

"Nae, lass, never intentionally."

His lips moved over hers, firm and warm. He tasted of

whisky, for what was a first-footing without whisky? He nudged her lips apart, and his tongue swept hers.

She parted her lips, welcoming the invasion, craving his warmth and taste.

Angling away, she smiled into his eyes, and her heart melted at the adoration she saw there. How humbling that this man loved her. A duke and a laird who could choose any woman had chosen her.

She took his hand and kissed the palm and then pressed her mouth to the back of the firm flesh. He smelled of horse, and leather, and Keane's unique rugged male essence.

A smattering of ebony hair tickled her nose, and she suspected the same dark hair covered much of his virile form. Damp heat pooled between her legs, and her mouth went dry at the delicious thought.

"I have an answer to the question you asked me earlier today," she said, else she yank him to the floor and have her way with him. Never had she hungered for a man, for the joining of their bodies, as she did for Keane. She was starving, and only he could satisfy her need.

Delight twinkled in his heavy-lidded hazel eyes sweeping down her scantily clad form. "Do ye now? And dare I hope 'tis an answer I shall like?"

She grinned as she uncurled her cramped legs and stood, reveling in the power of her womanhood. Relishing the knowledge that he wanted her as much as she wanted him.

"Aye, I think you'll be pleased," she said over her shoulder as she led him to the big, canopied bed. Every nerve vibrated with anticipation, lust, and love. So much love that tears pricked behind her eyelids and tightened her throat.

"Marjorie?" Keane's eyes had gone impossibly dark, the angles of his face etched in marble. "Ye've nae doubts? I willna deny I want ye so bad my body is afire for ye, but dinna do this out of gratitude. I'll wait until ye are ready, nae matter how long ye need, love. I'm nae a patient man, but for ye, I'll learn to be."

Marjorie smoothed a hand over the midnight stubble covering his hard jaw. She loved the sensation rasping against her palm, imagined that prickly beard abrading her as he pressed his mouth to her neck, her breasts, her belly... Everywhere.

Gratitude had nothing, *nothing*, to do with what they were about to do.

Lust and need and want and desire. *Aye, all of those.* But most of all, a soul-rendering love like she'd never known.

"I shall always and forever be grateful for what you did tonight, Keane, but this isn't about that. I want you in my bed, tonight and every night for as long as these Highlands exist. I want to give myself to you in body, in soul, and to take your name as mine."

"Och, *leannan.*" Issuing a guttural groan, half a sigh of relief and half a moan of pleasure, he swept her into his arms, tumbling them both onto the soft bed.

Playing her hands over the rigid curves and divots of his marvelous back and shoulders, she savored his weight pressing her into the soft mattress.

"I love ye, Marjorie."

He nuzzled the sensitive spot between her chin and collarbone and she giggled. "That tickles."

"Och, so the English lass is ticklish, is she?"

She nodded as she swept a lock of hair off his forehead. "Terribly, I fear."

His expression turned serious as his gaze fell on the chafed, red marks encircling her wrists. He brought each one to his mouth and pressed a reverent kiss to the damaged flesh. "When I saw ye tied, yer face bruised—"

She put two fingertips to his lips. "Shh. 'Tis over, and we are fine. I don't want to think about that right now. When I recall this Hogmanay, I want how much I love you and our first joining to be what comes to mind."

That was all the encouragement Keane needed. Between bold caresses and sizzling kisses, they stripped each other bare. She wasn't a shy maiden, but a woman who knew her body and a man's as well. Knew the pleasure that awaited them.

There wasn't any need for extended foreplay for Marjorie was ready for him, and given the heavy member jutting toward his taut belly, Keane was unquestionably ready for her as well.

They came together, swift and sure, her legs and womanhood open to him.

Both gasped aloud at Keane's initial penetration, and when completion hurtled them over the edge into bliss several minutes later, their simultaneous cries filled the chamber.

Afterward, as Marjorie lay satiated and content, her head upon Keane's shoulder and her eyes and limbs heavy with drowsiness, she kissed his chest. The broad, muscled expanse was, indeed, covered with fine, curly hair. Spreading her fingers wide, she combed through the soft mat.

"Yes," she murmured, her lips against his fragrant, warm skin.

God, he smelled splendid.

"Hmm?" Keane made a groggy sound deep in his throat. "Aye, what?"

"Yes, I'm sure I want to marry you."

A shudder rippled through him before he pulled her atop him, capturing her in a rather fierce embrace. "When?"

She chuckled and brushed that stubborn shock of hair off his forehead. "Is tomorrow too soon?"

"Nae for me, but I dinna want to rush ye, leannan."

"And I don't want another day to pass before I can call you my own."

"People will gossip, ye ken." His features sober, Keane trailed a finger across her collarbone. "They'll say we are foolish for rushin' into the union. Even yer family mightn't approve."

She rested her chin upon her hands, peering into his eyes. "I only care what you think, Keane."

He flashed a grin that scorched her to her toes. "I think we've wasted too much time already. When ye defied me last August, ye ignited a spark within my soul, and I have nae doubt that it will blaze hot and fierce for ye until I breathe my last."

"That's enough for me, my love," she murmured, settling upon him. "My very own Highland duke."

EPILOGUE

Trentwick Castle
May 1722

Arms clasped behind his back, Keane paced the corridor outside the bedchamber. Behind him, Elana and Cora, looking very much like angels in their lacy, white nightgowns, mimicked his actions. Chins tucked to their chests, their little arms behind their backs, they solemnly followed him.

Up and down. Up and down. Up and down.

Presently a small hand slipped into his, and he glanced down.

Cora peered up at him, her eyes trusting. "Papa, how much longer?"

"I'm no' sure, lass." And he wasn't. He'd never been through this before either.

Another small hand took possession of his other hand, and he winked at Elana.

"Come, let's sit for a spell, shall we?" he suggested. "I fear we've worn a path in the carpet."

They hadn't been waiting *that* long, but to the lasses, it undoubtedly seemed so.

Once settled on the floor across from the door, a wee lass tucked into each side, he rested his head against the wall.

Females certainly chose the worst times to give birth. Though he supposed the onset of labor at a quarter of ten wasn't as bad as it might've been, considering Marjorie had promised Elana and Cora they might stay up for the blessed event.

Anny exited the chamber, and they all perked up in expectation. Giving a rueful smile, she shook her head. "No' yet, but soon. Her Grace has requested tea and bread and jam. She says she's famished."

Marjorie was hungry at a time like this?

He'd have thought she'd be too busy with the birthing to eat, but what did he know of such matters?

"Can we have bread and jam and tea too, Papa?" Elana asked. "We can have a tea party out here while we wait."

Why not?

It was unlikely this glorious event would be over soon. If his daughters wanted a tea party this time of night, he'd happily oblige them. Marjorie regularly accused him of spoiling the lasses, and he supposed that was true.

He ought to have spoiled Branwen and Bethea more, and had he to do it over again, he wouldn't have been so protective. Och, who the hell was he trying to fool? He'd have been as protective, but he'd have permitted them more fun and perhaps a smidge more leniency.

But only a smidge.

Since they'd wed, he'd missed his wards more than he would've thought possible. They visited regularly and, try as he might, he still couldn't quite believe their choices of husbands.

"Anny, please bring enough for all of us," he said. "Mayhap shortbread and Scotch eggs if they are available too?"

Scotch eggs were a particular favorite of the lasses.

"Of course, Your Grace." A delighted smile brightening her face, Anny bustled away. The staff was continually amused at the doting papa he'd become.

Her head resting against his shoulder, Cora hummed beneath her breath while Elana walked her fingers up and down his forearm.

These darling girls and their mother had brought more peace and happiness into his life than he'd ever have imagined. He was happy, truly happy, and grew more so each day.

A few minutes later, just as Anny returned with the requested tea, the bedchamber door opened again. Phemie, grinning from ear to ear, poked her head out. "Ye can come in now."

Rather startled at the unexpectedly swift birth, Keane rose.

Elana and Cora had already scampered to their feet and darted to the door where they bounced on their toes.

He held his hands out and wiggled his fingers, and they obediently latched onto him. "We shall need to be verra quiet and calm. Newborns are verra sensitive to noise."

"Aye, we'll be as quiet as mouses," Cora whispered.

"Mice," Elana corrected, in the way only an older sister could.

Perplexed, Cora frowned. "That's what I said, Elana. Mouses."

Elana rolled her eyes and looked to Keane for confirmation.

"Let's go in, shall we?" he suggested.

The girls nodded eagerly, and when Phemie swung the door wide, they both tip-toed inside.

Anny followed, bearing the laden tray. "Shall I lay it out on the table, Your Grace?"

Marjorie glanced up from the basket she'd been peering into atop the bed. "Yes, please." As the maid set the service on the table, Marjorie waved her daughters forward. "Come, darlings."

They released his hands and ran to the bed, scrambling onto the mattress.

"Gently," their mother warned softly.

"Ooh," Cora breathed reverently.

Elana gasped. "Three?"

Keane neared the bed, his heart swelling at the wonderment in the girls' faces.

"Papa." Cora looked up, awe stamped upon her features. "Chimera had *three* kittens."

Eyes half-closed, Chimera relaxed on her side, three tiny bits of fuzz suckling at her teats. Sphynx leaped onto the bed, evidently curious what the fuss was all about.

She sniffed each kitten, then nosed her sister in approval before plopping her very rounded form beside the basket. She'd deliver her bairns soon too. In truth, he'd expected the cats to have become mothers long ago.

Likely, that dapper black fellow with the white whiskers and mustache that had shown up around the stables a few months back was responsible for Chimera and Sphynx's condition.

A light rap at the door preceded Nurse Swinton's entrance, an ebony-haired bundle cuddled in her plump arms. "The wee master is awake, and the little rogue is tryin' to convince me he hasna eaten in a fortnight. I wasna sure whether ye wanted me to bring him here or to yer bedchamber."

Keane assisted Marjorie off the bed, and she gathered their seven-month-old son into her arms.

"Here is just fine." She angled her head toward the basket. "We have three new members of the household."

"Och, now that's a blessin', to be sure," Nurse said with the perfect blend of awe and reverence.

Already Cora and Elana were discussing appropriate names for the wee mites.

Keane whispered in Marjorie's ear. "We're no' going to be keepin' all of them, are we?"

A winsome smile playing about her pretty mouth, she lifted her shoulder.

That would be a yes.

"All right, darlings," she said. "'Tis far past your bedtime. Go along to bed now, and when I've finished feeding Parker, Papa and I will tuck you in."

With obvious reluctance, the girls climbed off the bed, but their expressions changed to adoration when their mother bent so they could kiss their baby brother's soft cheek.

"Good night, Parker," Cora said, poking a finger into his tiny fist. "Sleep well. Tomorrow ye can meet the new kitties."

"Good night, little brother." Elana ran her hand over his shock of thick hair.

Keane bent and kissed the crown of each of their heads. "Good night, sweetlin's."

"Good night, Papa," Cora murmured, rubbing her fists into her eyes.

"Will the kittens be allowed to sleep with us soon?" Elana asked over a yawn.

"Not until they are bigger." Marjorie shook her head. "It

wouldn't be safe for them. And Chimera will not want to leave her bairns, so you'll have to be patient."

"Come along, pets," Nurse encouraged with an indulgent smile, and the girls accepted her outstretched hands. "Phemie, once the little misses are abed, I'll have ye sit with them while I collect the wee master."

They were between governesses again. The last had married the blacksmith, so Marjorie had posted adverts once more.

After everyone had left, Marjorie put Parker to her breast. He gazed at her in the way only an infant enamored of their mother can, but now and again he veered his gaze to Keane. He had his mother's deep brown eyes.

Suddenly, he grinned around the nipple in his mouth, and Keane's heart toppled over as he fell in love with his son all over again.

With an arm around Marjorie's shoulders, they took a final look at the contentedly sleeping cats before making their way to the chamber they'd shared since that splendid night she'd said she'd be his for all time.

Once inside, Keane took his now sleeping son from Marjorie's arms. He kissed Parker's soft, smooth forehead, breathing in his sweet scent. "I never kent I could be this happy."

Marjorie slipped an arm about his torso, their son between them. "I'm tempted to believe Dolag's prediction of tremendous peace, happiness, and prosperity, for certainly we've been blessed with that and more."

"Aye, my love, we have." He kissed her temple. "I believe 'tis because a redhaired siren consented to be my wife and brought me, my clan, and the duchy more good fortune than a thousand men might experience."

She sighed and smiled, resting her head against his shoulder. "You, husband, sound like a man completely besotted."

"Aye, that I am."

If you'd like to leave a review, please scan the QR code.

Keep reading for a free preview of
TO MARRY A HIGHLAND MARAUDER
Heart of a Scot Series, Book Seven

Earl of Monteith's Ball
Edinburgh, Scotland
21 March 1721

Peeking around a Grecian column, Bethea Glanville warily scanned the illustrious assemblage. Elaborately attired, self-important gentlemen and ladies dripping in satin, velvet, every manner of jewel imaginable, and gasp-worthy towering wigs packed the breathtaking but overly-crowded ballroom.

One grand dame required two attendants, one on either side, to guide her around. Her pink ribbon-adorned white wig contained a birdcage—complete with a live and petrified-looking canary. She could scarcely move her head lest the creation either topple from her head or send her tumbling ample bosom over abundant bum.

Bethea couldn't help but wonder what would happen if the bird needed to relieve its wee self, and despite the direness of her situation, a naughty grin momentarily twitched her mouth.

Until now, she'd never considered herself a coward. She

enjoyed challenges, meeting new people, and experiencing new things. Yet the past fortnight, she'd done her utmost to avoid an amorous lord's wholly unwanted attentions.

Only now, she had begun skulking behind potted greeneries, diving into curtained alcoves, and made so many excuses to seek the lady's retiring room that people might've begun pondering if a health condition plagued her.

Odin's gnarly teeth. How had she ever thought *this* was what she wanted?

How many times had she and her sister, Branwen, complained to their guardian, Keane Buchannan, Duke of Roxdale, that he was too strict and protective? That they longed to attend elaborate fetes and soirees such as this very ball? That at one and twenty, she was of marriageable age, and she wanted to fall in love, marry, and have children?

Well, not precisely this minute or week or month even, but in due course.

In truth, Bethea thoroughly enjoyed the dancing and the gaiety. The musical performances, teas, and all the rest were exhausting but exciting, nonetheless. Though she wasn't the belle of any ball, enough gentlemen had asked her to dance and otherwise paid her pretty compliments that she had a grand time thus far.

When noxious David Talbot, Earl of Monteith, wasn't following her and sniffing about her skirts, that was. Rarely— never before, in truth— had she met anyone as off-putting and as persistent as the earl. He was worse than a ratty terrier after a meaty bone.

Pursing her mouth at the thought, Bethea stood on her tiptoes, craning her neck to see over the milling merrymakers and dancers. Tonight's assembled were some of the most extravagant she'd seen, and she couldn't help but be slightly impressed at the earl's scope of influence—even if she intensely disliked the man himself.

Where are they?

She gripped the column tighter, scrutinizing the undulating crowd which seemed to have swallowed her sister, Keane, and his lovely new wife, Marjorie.

Wait. Squinting, Bethea arched even higher on her toes. *Is that...?* For an elated instant, she hoped she'd spotted a familiar raven head, shoulders above the milling assemblage.

Was Camden Kennedy here?

The notion caused a little thrill of excitement to rush through her, immediately followed by her knitting her eyebrows together into a perplexed vee.

Odd, but neither Keane nor Marjorie had mentioned that Camden—one of her first husband's brothers—was even in Edinburgh, let alone expected here tonight.

In a blink, the throng shifted, obstructing whoever the man was from her avid view. Inexplicable disappointment swept Bethea. She'd very much wanted him to be Camden Kennedy.

Standing well over six feet, all brawn and muscle, but with a perpetual twinkle in his vivid blue eyes, Camden would've kept her safe from Monteith. Now *there* was a man she could trust not to impose himself on her. Not once in the times that she'd encountered Camden had he stepped beyond the mark in word or action.

A practiced flirt possessing a disarming wit, he usually made her laugh too.

A heavy-treaded, unsteady *clickety-clop, clickety-clop* announced the Earl of Monteith's approach before she smelled the perpetually malodorous man.

Lovely.

Daring another peek, she stifled a distressed gasp.

Drat, drat, and double drat-damn.

The very man she'd managed to avoid the past hour toddled toward her on absurdly embellished blue and silver high-heeled shoes, perspiration profusely beading the wide expanse of his brow and upper lip. His ridiculously curled wig brushed his shoulders, and she strongly suspected a number of vermin made the wig their home. The engraved, shiny silver buttons fastened across his stomach strained to contain his corpulence.

By all the saints, if he sneezed, the fastenings would become lethal projectiles.

Her mouth quivered again at the image of the prestigious guests in attendance laid out flat by flying buttons.

Her mirth, however, was short-lived.

The Earl of Monteith, and her host for this evening, had found her. *Again.* The nobleman was persistent, if nothing else. No amount of politely discouraging the middling-aged man's attentions deterred him from his pointed pursuit of her since her family had arrived in Edinburgh.

Tattle had it, he was in the market for a countess, and apparently, he'd set his bleary, dumpling-eyed sights on her. Bethea had done nothing to encourage his interest, and the more she attempted to put him off, the more determined he had become to seek her out. Like a great perspiring and smelly hound on the scent.

If he hadn't already, she truly feared Monteith meant to ask Keane for her hand.

God save her from such a horrific fate.

A shudder rippled up her spine, spreading out in prickly waves across her shoulders and tingling her scalp. The very notion made the small midday meal she'd consumed threaten to reappear.

Swallowing, Bethea pressed a hand to her middle, willing the queasiness roiling there to abate.

Keane wouldn't betroth her without telling her.

She had no doubt of that, and Marjorie well knew Bethea and Branwen desired a love-match. A widowed Englishwoman, Marjorie had become the older sister Bethea had never had, and both she and Branwen had confided their dreams and fears to her.

A curious, rather austere lady caught her peeping around the column, and Bethea couldn't resist a mischievous little finger wave. When the woman promptly elevated her reedy nose and turned her back in a direct snub, Bethea chuckled. Only since arriving in Edinburgh and experiencing the—ah— *flamboyant* and—ah—*interesting* persons of elevated station had this peculiar bend toward precociousness overcome her.

Standing on her toes again, Bethea desperately searched the room for Branwen, Keane, or Marjorie. She didn't know anyone else well enough to approach them. *If only that had been Camden Kennedy.* In truth, she shouldn't be hiding here alone. There were those only too eager to cast aspersions on something as innocent as an unchaperoned lass.

And I was so eager to experience High Society.

Bethea huffed a rude noise beneath her breath, not daring to voice the unladylike oath she wasn't even supposed to know, let alone utter.

Bent on a hasty retreat, she gathered the iridescent silver and lavender of her satin gown in her gloved hands. She might very well heave decorum aside and cause a scandal by hiking her skirts to her knees and sprinting across the room. Anything to avoid Monteith.

How she wished she was back at Trentwick Castle in the Highlands right now. Boredom was, indeed, preferable to hiding at every event and dreading an unwanted proposal.

She cast another desperate glance about the ballroom.

Praise the heavens.

There Marjorie was. Her fiery red tresses were a much welcome, glowing beacon.

"Miss Glanville," the earl puffed breathlessly from several paces away.

Och, hell in a basket.

Determined to avoid a dance as unpleasant as the one she'd suffered through at the Cavendishs' two nights ago, Bethea pretended not to hear him. His fetid scent had compelled her to hold her breath each time the reel's steps forced them together. Without glancing behind her, she dove into the throng, winding her way through the guests.

Several people smiled or inclined their heads—two or three gentlemen quite lecherously—but mindful of Marjorie's instruction, Bethea maintained an air of genial indifference as she swiftly wove through the colorful tapestry of people. The instinct to run, to put as much distance as possible between herself and the Earl of Monteith, thrummed through her.

Nevertheless, she kept her pace brisk yet modulated.

"At all times, present yourselves as polite and approachable, but not eager or forward," Marjorie had counseled her and Branwen when Keane had, at last, conceded to present them in Edinburgh. "A young lady must act agreeable without seeming overly-friendly toward any gentlemen. A very fine line exists between politesse and what some consider fast or impudent behavior," Marjorie had solemnly advised.

No doubt, naughtily waving at a busybody fell into the latter category.

So many ridiculous rules to observe, half of which, Marjorie and Keane dolefully acknowledged, changed on a whim.

Be reserved, but not austere.

Smile, but not coyly.

Exemplify graciousness, but do not encourage or tolerate scandalous behavior.

And on and on and on and *on* went the list of strictures and expectations. How could anyone possibly be themselves?

No wonder Keane hadn't been enthusiastic about toting them to Edinburgh and enduring the social scene. A constant, unnerving undercurrent hummed beneath the outward facades of geniality, and Bethea had already learned not to take anyone at their word.

Pulse high and breathing erratic from the discomfiture the Earl of Monteith always roused, Bethea tried not to draw undue attention as she slowed her steps to a sedate pace and approached Marjorie.

Attired in a stunning sea-green gown that set off her bronze hair to perfection, she chatted with a trio of attractive ladies. Marjorie spied her, and producing a welcoming smile, she extended her hand and drew Bethea near her. Her treacle-brown gaze gravitated past Bethea, and flexing the merest bit, comprehension dawned in the depths of her eyes.

Perfect. Just as Bethea had hoped.

Aye, Keane had made a brilliant choice in selecting this exceptional woman for his duchess. Not only was she warm and loving, but her two adorable daughters had brought much laughter to the keep.

"Your sister is dancing at the moment," Marjorie said in her lilting English accent, one eye trained on Monteith's laborious progress. "And Keane excused himself a few minutes ago and left the ballroom with Mr. Frederick Rickerson and the Marquis of Pennsworth." Jollity shone in her eyes. "They claimed they had important *business* to discuss."

One of the other women, a petite brunette with a shy smile, chuckled and arched an eyebrow. Lady Abagail

Fitzpatrick, if Bethea recalled correctly. "Which means they stole off to have a stiff drink. No doubt to congratulate Roxdale for having the good sense to marry you, Your Grace."

Before Marjorie had a chance to introduce Bethea to the other pair, Monteith was upon them. Except for Marjorie, the ladies dipped into perfunctory curtsies, though she angled her head. She outranked him but nonetheless curved her mouth into a gracious smile. Her nose only twitched the merest bit as his overpowering stench wafted near.

Bethea wouldn't even permit her imagination to conjure up an image of what bedding him would entail. *You needn't fear on that account*, she reminded herself. Keane would never consent to such a match.

Would he?

She bit her lower lip, traitorous uncertainty pricking her.

He was most determined to improve the duchy's standing and reputation, and if one of his wards were to marry a powerful earl...

Nae. I shallna think of it.

Lady Fitzpatrick promptly snapped her fan open and went about creating a vigorous breeze as the other two women surreptitiously stepped backward a few paces. It said much about Monteith's sphere of influence that so many guests graced his ballroom, despite his hygiene issue.

Did Monteith truly have no knowledge of how offensive his body odor was?

Perhaps he had an unfortunate condition that caused the malodorousness.

Why else would he not address the embarrassing matter?

"Yer Grace, might I call upon ye and His Grace tomorrow afternoon?" Monteith half-wheezed, sending Bethea a sly look from beneath his heavily hooded gaze. His smile crinkled the fleshy, wrinkled pouches drooping beneath his eyes. "I have a matter of some import I wish to discuss with him. A matter I'm confident he'll be amenable to."

Good God! Nae.

Bethea's heart stopped beating before plummeting straight to her lavender silk shoes. Her throat went dry as hot sand, and an icy chill swamped her.

It was just as she'd feared.

He intended to ask Keane for her hand in marriage.

Marjorie still held her hand, and Bethea squeezed hard, sending a silent, panicked message.

Monteith had some nerve cornering Marjorie when others were present, thereby making the refusal of his request more awkward. The boor should've sent a card around requesting an audience. However, Bethea had learned another thing about Monteith: no one's opinion of him exceeded his own.

Please say nae. Please say nae, she mentally chanted, hoping her eyes didn't reveal her absolute desperation. The fact that every ounce of blood in her body had drained to her toes wouldn't give her away either.

"I regret we shan't be home tomorrow," Marjorie said coolly with the perfect combination of solicitousness and inflexibility. And praise the saints, she didn't offer an explanation as to where they would be, for the earl was brazen enough to put in an appearance.

Thank God.

Marjorie serenely scanned the ballroom before returning her attention to him. "I see this set has ended, my lord, and my husband's other ward is searching for us. I take my role as chaperone very seriously and must make my way to her, your lordship. Please excuse us."

A tinge of steel threaded her last words.

With a cordial nod to the ladies, each of their expressions

schooled into blandness but a knowing glint in their eyes, she led Bethea away.

"Has he been pestering you, Bethea?" Marjorie asked beneath her breath as they fell into step, putting several feet between themselves and the pungent earl.

"Aye, and I can scarcely relax and enjoy myself. I've taken to hidin' or lurkin' in shadows. Monteith makes my skin crawl." Bethea extracted her hand and then fitted it into Marjorie's bent arm. "I fear he means to propose, and I canna abide him, Marjorie." A note of anxiousness crept into her voice. "Keane wouldna—"

"Lord have mercy, no." Marjorie gave a vigorous shake of her head. "Never think it, my dear. He thinks Monteith's a sweaty toad, but the earl does have valuable connections. We'll need to put Monteith off without offending him. I've already extracted a promise from Keane that you and Branwen will have your choice of husbands."

"Have I told ye how glad I am Keane married ye?" Bethea pressed nearer to Marjorie's side, a wide grin arcing her mouth. "I didna ken how we managed without ye before."

Marjorie squeezed her arm. "And I'm delighted he has wards who could be the younger sisters I never had."

They were upon Branwen now, resplendent in midnight blue and white. Her stance uneven, she offered a pained smile. "I fear my last partner trod upon my feet so many times that my toes are severely bruised. I believe I'll rest for a few minutes in the ladies' retirin' room. Hopefully, puttin' my feet up will do the trick."

"I'll go with ye," Bethea offered, seizing the excuse to help her sister and avoid Monteith.

Marjorie nodded. "I'll let Keane know."

"Ah, there you are, Marjorie." A pretty, plump woman with light brown hair and a radiant smile approached. "I've been searching for you all evening." Her curious gaze gravitated to Bethea and her sister. "And these must be Keane's wards."

"Anna, I didn't know you were in Scotland." Marjorie bussed her cheek. "Yes, this is Bethea." She indicated Bethea with a sweep of her hand. "And Branwen Glanville. Girls, this is Anna Buchannan Hawthorne. She's actually a second or third cousin to Keane. We were girlhood friends."

Anna laughed, a merry twinkle in her pale brown eyes. "Well, my branch of the family rarely ventured north of the border, and that's why I've never met you in all this time."

"'Tis a pleasure," Bethea greeted. "How wonderful that ye were friends, and now ye're cousins."

"Indeed," Branwen agreed, shifting on her feet and grimacing slightly.

She truly was uncomfortable.

Marjorie linked her elbow with Anna's. "The girls were just on their way to the retiring room, but why don't we find a quiet corner and catch up?"

"A splendid idea," Anna agreed. "Ten years is far too long."

"I'll come for you in half an hour," Marjorie told Bethea and Branwen before turning away, her coppery head bent to hear what Anna was saying.

Bethea promptly wrapped an arm around Branwen's waist and slowly guided her slightly taller sister from the ballroom. Though Branwen put on a brave face, her pinched lips and occasional flinches revealed the state of her damaged feet.

Ladies ought to be warned of Lord Hurstwood's proclivity to mash his partners' feet.

"Ye poor darlin'," Bethea murmured as they entered the corridor.

"Lord Hurstwood is an exuberant dance partner, and I

vow he tromped upon my toes a score of times." Branwen winced again, and a small gasp escaped her.

Lord Hurstwood was no small man either. Not given to corpulence like Monteith, Hurstwood was nonetheless a thick, stocky sort an inch or two over six feet.

Alarm spiked in Bethea.

Just how badly injured were Branwen's feet?

Bethea's scalp tingled, and she had the unmistakable sensation that someone watched her. As she turned the corner, she cut a swift glance along the passage. Her flesh puckered when she spotted the Earl of Monteith, his bulbous form framed in the ballroom's entrance, staring at her with unfettered lust upon his fleshy face.

A sly smile curved his full mouth, and he boldly winked.

Just as she jerked her focus away, Camden Kennedy's massive form appeared behind the earl. He looked straight at her, and a scintillating current sparked between them.

He is *here.*

When had he arrived?

And more mystifying, why hadn't he sought her family out?

I hope you enjoyed this free preview of
TO MARRY A HIGHLAND MARAUDER
Heart of a Scot
Book Seven

FREE PREVIEW

Thank you for reading TO DEFY A HIGHLAND DUKE. Marjorie and Keane took me on a few twists and turns I hadn't seen coming, but it was their story, so I let them have fun.

Prior research had introduced me to Scottish Wildcats, and I found the creatures fascinating. I assumed they were similar to feral cats, and while they do breed with other species, the true Scottish Wildcat prefers woodlands to grasslands. They are also bigger than I'd first imagined. Skeletal remains indicate the cats, thought to have descended from European wildcats, can measure five feet from tip of tail to tip of nose. The average domesticated cat is eighteen inches in length, not including its tail.

For those of you not aware, Scots didn't openly acknowledge Christmas during the 18th century, but Hogmanay was, and still is, a time of great revelry. First-footing is a favorite tradition, and if a tall, dark-haired man was the first to cross a threshold in the new year, that household was guaranteed good luck. I wasn't able to find specifics regarding the reading of hearth ashes, also called redding. My research mentioned this as an ancient Hogmanay tradition, and I confess to a bit of author creativity in that regard.

I truly hope you found a few hours of relaxation, escaping to the 18th century Highlands with Marjorie and Keane. If so, be sure to check out the other books in my HEART OF A SCOT series.

To make sure you don't miss any of my book news, subscribe to my newsletter (Get a free book too!). I also have a fabulous VIP Reader Group on Facebook, Collette Chéris. If you're a fan of my books and historical romance, I'd love to have you join me. You'll also be the first to see new covers, read exclusive excerpts, be the first to know about contests and give-aways, help me pick titles and name characters, and much, much more.

Please consider telling other readers why you enjoyed this book by reviewing it as well. I also truly adore hearing from my readers. You can contact me on my www.collettecameron-books.com and while you are there, explore my author world.

Hugs,
Collette

If you haven't joined Collette's exclusive mailing list click on QR image to sign up! You'll get access to exclusive content, sneak peeks, contests, giveaways, and more...

(P.S. No spam!)

https://collettecameronbooks.com/freegift

Collette loves to hear from readers.
You can contact her via her website: collettecameron-books.com.
Or email her directly at collette@collettecameron-books.com.

You can also follow Collette on social media:
Facebook: https://www.-facebook.com/ColletteCameronNovels/
Instagram: https://instagram.com/collettecameronauthor/
Goodreads: https://www.goodreads.com/collettecameron
Book Bub: https://www.bookbub.com/authors/collette-cameron

Pinterest: http://www.pinterest.com/colletteauthor/
YouTube: https://www.youtube.com/@ColletteCamero-
nAuthor

Giggles are Guaranteed
Collette's Cheris Reader Group

https://www.facebook.com/groups/CollettesCheris/

If you love to chat about all things romance-book related and enjoy taking part in fun and engaging live events, contests, and giveaways join **Collette's Chèris VIP Reader Group, https://www.facebook.com/groups/CollettesCheris/,** my exclusive private book group on Facebook.

Giggles are guaranteed!

Hope to see you there,
Collette Cameron®

ABOUT THE AUTHOR

COLLETTE CAMERON®

USA Today Bestselling author Collette Cameron® is renowned for her captivating, humorous, and heartwarming Scottish and Regency historical romance novels. With over 65 published titles, over 1.6 million books sold around the world, and multiple writing awards to her credit, Collette is a well-known author in the world of historical romance.

Readers love her witty and relatable characters including daring rogues, dashing scoundrels, and the strong and spirited heroines who capture their hearts. From the rugged highlands to the refined drawing rooms of Regency England, Collette's novels will transport you to another time and place, where love and adventure are just a page away.

Collette's Sweet-to-Spicy Timeless Romances® are the perfect escape for readers looking for romantic escape, poignant inspiration, engaging humor, and entertaining stories.

Based in the Pacific Northwest, Collette is surrounded by the lush greenery and rainy skies that inspire her writing. She dreams of one day splitting her time between the Pacific Northwest and Scotland. In the meantime, she indulges in her love of all things cobalt blue, dachshunds, chocolate, and of course, crafting her next historical romance.

Blue Rose Romance® LLC
collette@collettecameronbooks.com
collettecameronbooks.com

ALSO BY COLLETTE CAMERON®

BLUE ROSE ROMANCE® LLC
COLLETTE CAMERON'S® COMPLETE BOOK LIST

CHRONICLES OF THE WESTBROOK BRIDES
A Romantic Opposites Attract Mystery & Suspense
Family Saga Regency Romance

Midnight Christmas Waltz — *Book 1*

Mission at Midnight — *Book 2*

The Midnight Marquess — *Book 3*

Holly, Mistletoe, and Midnight Snow — *Book 4*

The Wallflower's Midnight Waltz — *Book 5*

Minuet at Midnight — *Book 6*

Kiss a Rake at Midnight — *Book 7*

Unmasked at Midnight — *Book 8*

Memories Made at Midnight — *Book 9*

Once Upon a Midnight Dream — *Book 10*

DUKES COME CALLING
A Sensual Marriage of Convenience
Regency Historical Romance

A Diamond for a Duke — *Book 1*

Only a Duke Would Dare — *Book 2*

A December with a Duke — Book 3

What Would a Duke Do? — Book 4

Wooed by a Wicked Duke — Book 5

Duchess of His Heart — Book 6

Never Dance with a Duke — Book 7

Wedding Her Christmas Duke — Book 8

The Debutante and the Duke — Book 9

Loved by a Dangerous Duke — Book 10

How to Win a Duke's Heart — Book 11

When a Duke Desires a Lass — Book 12

My Dearest Duke — Book 13

~

FOR THE LOVE OF AN EARL (Wicked Earls' Club)
A Humorous Aristocrat and Wallflower
Regency Romance Adventure

Earl of Wainthorpe — Book 1

Earl of Scarborough — Book 2

Earl of Keyworth — Book 3

Earl of Renshaw — Book 4

~

HEART OF A SCOT
A Passionate Enemies to Lovers
Scottish Highlander Historical Mystery
Romance Adventure

HIGHLAND HEATHER ROMANCING A SCOT: CASTLE BRIDES

A Passionate Enemies to Lovers Second Chance

Scottish Highlander Mystery Romance

~

LADIES OF OPPORTUNITY
A Bluestockings and Rogues Opposites Attract
Regency Mystery Christmas Romance

The Wallflower's Wild Wager — Book 1

The Spinster's Secret Stake, Book 2

Better Not Bet a Bluestocking – Book 3

~

SECRETS OF SCANDALOUS LADIES
A Romantic Class Difference Forced Proximity
Regency Romance with Aristocrats

A Lady's Scandalous Kiss — Book 1

No Lady for the Lord — Book 2

Love Lessons for a Lady — Book 3

His One and Only Lady — Book 4

Never a Proper Lady — Book 5

Lady Tempts a Rogue — Book 6

~

THE CULPEPPER MISSES
A Humorous Wallflower Family Saga
Regency Romantic Comedy

The Earl and the Spinster — Book 1

The Marquis and the Vixen — Book 2

THE HONORABLE ROGUES®
A Second Chance Redeemable Rogue
and Wallflower Regency Romance